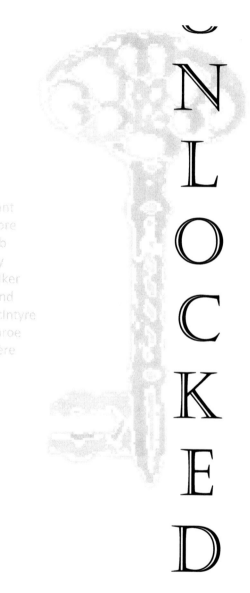

Jaimey Grant
Wendy Swore
Rita Webb
Paige Ray
Jeanne Voelker
K. G. Borland
Gwendolyn McIntyre
Katrina Monroe
S. M. Carrière

# UNLOCKED

First published by Wendy Swore & Rita J. Webb in 2010

All rights reserved. Published in the United States by Wendy Swore and Rita J. Webb and printed by CreateSpace.com.

ISBN: 1453756426
EAN-13: 9781453756423.

Edited by Wendy Swore and Rita J. Webb.
Page layout by Rita J. Webb.
Cover photos by Wendy Swore.
Cover design by Laura J. Miller.

UnlockedProject.com
UnlockedProject.blogspot.com

# TABLE OF CONTENTS

*Dedicated to all who read,*
*for reading is the key*
*to unlocking your dreams.*

I walk down a long, dark corridor filled with doors. Clutched in my hand is a ring of keys of various sizes and shapes and colors. Each key will open a door, some leading to new worlds, others hiding secrets better left forgotten, and still more holding dreams to be shared.

At the end of the hall stands a wooden chest with a golden latch. I fumble through my keys and insert one after another until the lock clicks softly. The lid feels heavy in my hand as I push it open.

Something wrapped in a cloth lies in the bottom of the chest. Carefully opening the cloth, I find a book. Is it a book of stories or a guide to my key ring? Why is the book locked away? Is it precious or might it be dangerous?

In golden letters, one word is engraved across the leather cover: *Unlocked*.

# ASSASSIN'S KEEPER
## Jaimey Grant

*It's his job to clean up her messes.*

It was almost too easy.

Sable hated it when a killing went too smoothly. It was like thumbing one's nose at the devil, taunting him to do his worst. She'd experienced the devil's worst and had since made it her goal to never live through that again.

Staring down into the now sightless eyes of her latest mark, Sable felt a faint satisfaction that the deed was done. Death seemed a normal part of life these days, for everyone. It made little difference if she helped a few along their way to meet their maker—or to a far more deserving hell.

She nudged the body on the floor with her foot. The man, once so handsome and charming, smiled now in eternal sleep. His reign of terror was over; he'd raped his last helpless woman.

Being a rapist was a suitable reason to die. Sable had killed for less. The bloodlust firing her very existence simmered deep inside.

Instinct flared, warning of danger. Another presence lingered, just beyond the study door. Nervous fear swept her spine. She backed away from the dead man, each methodical step falling with utter silence on the carpeted floor.

Tilting her head, she filtered out the usual London night sounds. Carriage wheels on cobblestones, clinking harnesses, and barking dogs—all faded into the back of her mind. She listened for anything out of the ordinary.

There: a nearly inaudible step.

Pushing back into the shadows, Sable waited.

The minutes crept by. Each passing second brought her closer to discovery. She hated unnecessary killings. An unfortunate servant or two had met their ends after stumbling upon a death scene before Sable completed her mission. She couldn't ignore the very real threat they represented.

The creak of the door snared her full attention. Somebody entered, looked down at the body and...just stood there. Then, moving with nearly as much stealth as herself, the man approached the open window and stared out into the starless night.

Sable poised on the balls of her feet, ready to strike. Just as she moved to lunge, something in the man's stance warned her she might not come out of this confrontation the winner.

She checked her movement, easing along the shadows to the open door. She had to escape. Something about the man made her skin crawl, as if she were not the only evil in the room.

As she slipped through the portal, she heard a low, faintly accented voice say, "Very good, Sable. But did you have to shed quite so much blood?"

She cursed. Without a thought for the consequences, she picked up a heavy figurine from the table by the door and hurled it at the man who'd been ordered to spy on her.

He turned and caught the object. Sable ignored her moment of shock and escaped before he could overcome his.

A vile curse floated on the misty, early-morning air. The man at the window shoved a hand through his dark blond hair as yet another vulgarity passed his lips.

Part of him wanted to go after her, but he didn't have time. He was supposed to make her crime seem like robbery, suicide, or an accident. Staring at the bloody body on the floor, he chose robbery. After a half-hearted inquest and no killer to find, the authorities would abandon the case.

Sable's real identity remained a mystery to his superiors. They took her in after she committed the most gruesome murder he could ever recall. Her lack of remorse coupled with her intriguing methods led them to offer her the most despised and dangerous occupation ever devised—paid assassin.

And she was good. Damn good. It was nothing short of a miracle that he'd managed to stumble across her before she'd left.

He set about his business. She excelled at her job and he excelled at his. He understood her need to use a knife on this particular mark but he wished she'd used a pistol instead. Had she shot the man, he could have made it look like suicide. Suicide was an easier answer when setting up a crime scene as the authorities enjoyed a certain notoriety for their lax investigation of such crimes.

As he turned to leave, something glinted in the moonlight filtering through the window. He stooped, sweeping up a small key. The broken chain dangled over his wrist. Sable's trinket, no doubt. He'd caught a glimpse of it earlier, the chain around her neck and the key disappearing beneath her bodice as she dressed for a ball. Suspicions aroused at her decision to even attend such a gathering, he'd been sent to discover what drew her to the glittering mass of Society at play.

That night took her to Carleton House where she'd flirted with the Prince Regent and made a general spectacle of herself. Her beauty and wealth afforded her entrée to the most elite of homes. Masquerading as any lady, her killer instinct led her to the gatherings harboring a worthy kill. The dead man on the floor had attended the same ball.

Sable culled her marks from under Society's very nose.

His fingers clenched around the bauble, the key's sharp teeth pressing into his palm. He alone knew how deep Sable's vengeance ran. She would do anything to kill a mark, whether that person was assigned or one of her own choosing. His superiors' tolerance would only last until they realized how uncontrollable she was. Then her elimination would be *his* next assignment.

A smile threatened. He had managed to annoy her. His superiors questioned her humanity, but he knew beyond doubt that somewhere under that lethal exterior beat the heart of a passionate woman. Her loss of composure at his unexpected appearance proved it.

And a human being could be exploited. It was only a matter of time before she became their weakness rather than their strength.

As the assassin's keeper, it was his job to clean up the mess.

As she vaulted across slippery London rooftops, contempt and fury roiled in her center at the thought of her midnight guest. Bloody French rat. The slightest trace of Paris crept along his softly uttered words like a snake ready to strike. The dulcet tones filled her with such rage she'd acted without thought, something she hadn't done since...

With a violent shake of her head, Sable flew across the last rooftop before reaching her destination. Concentrating on her actions, she slithered along the edge of the roof, dropping with infinite grace onto a very slim ledge. Swinging through the open window, she landed on her feet.

The room lay wreathed in shadows. She didn't bother with a lamp. She lived her life in darkness and preferred it that way. Shedding her gloves and short cape, she moved across the floor toward the door on the other side.

She lived alone, had no friends or acquaintances. Between marks, she had plenty of time to think, and too often, her thoughts turned inward.

Thinking was not a pastime she enjoyed.

But then, her life offered little enjoyment.

With a small shake of her head, she tossed her black shirt away and shed her tight trousers. They landed on the floor by her bed in a heap. Dejected. Alone.

In the beginning, she'd been so bent on vengeance that she'd given little or no thought to how she'd feel when her revenge was accomplished. After her first blundering attempt to assassinate the man responsible for her parents' deaths, she'd honed her skills and made it her life's work to rid the world of the scum who masqueraded as honorable nobility. But unlike the revolutionary leaders of France, she'd done her research, seeking only those whose crimes went unpunished, whose guilt was so apparent that even a jury would be unable to claim otherwise. How ironic that a simple servant had managed to take her down, if only temporarily. Then she'd been condemned for her "crimes" and rescued by the man who now liked to think he owned her.

Unfortunately, he did.

She shrugged into a dressing gown, her movements unusually jerky. Lowering herself into a chair, she forced calm over herself and carefully undid the pins in her hair, a vanity she could ill-afford. She really should cut off the bloody dark tresses.

Sable shook her head. Waves of black floated around her. At the thought of her unexpected visitor, an ache she hadn't felt since watching her parents die settled in her chest.

Lord Castlereagh had sent her keeper to determine if she was still an asset to the Regent's government. Not that the Regent knew anything of the matter. What the ruler didn't know he could deny with absolute honesty.

Her keeper. As if she needed a man to tell her what to do! Yet, that was exactly what her life had become. Cursing, she grabbed the first thing at hand. A heavy silver mirror sailed across the room. The crash of glass shattered the night, pieces of the wreckage winking back at her in the moonbeams from her open window.

She ignored them, her fingers reaching for the key she always wore. It was her one comfort, a reminder of who and what she was, where she came from and where she was going. It was the only thing she loved.

It was gone!

Panic flared, an all-consuming tightening in her chest that threatened to burst. In overlooking the key's absence, she'd lost the most important piece of herself.

It could be anywhere. Rising, her eyes darted around the dim chamber, seeking a miracle in the black corners, but life had taught her that miracles didn't exist for one such as she.

Searching her room with a frenzy her keeper would not have recognized, Sable came to the horrible conclusion she'd lost it somewhere out in the night. Leaning so far out the window that an ordinary person might have fallen, her eyes probed the darkness, seeking out any slight glimmer of moonlight on metal.

Nothing. Defeated, Sable moved to her bed, her gaze settling on the slight depression in the other pillow. Her anger dulled with weariness and despair. She composed her mind for sleep, a difficult task that saw success hours later.

Not quite the obedient little subordinate he pretended to be, Etienne du Clerc knew how to play the game. When Lord Castlereagh demanded his presence, he nodded and agreed just as if he cared one jot what the man said.

"Furthermore, I want you to nullify the problem. Sable has gone too far. She takes for granted the patronage of this government and that must be rectified."

Etienne nodded. "As you wish, my lord. Shall you be requiring her head on a pike?"

"Take care lest you find your own head on a pike, sir."

Etienne's less than respectful response was in French, further angering his lordship. Perhaps not the wisest course, but one he could not resist. Etienne could not easily accept Castlereagh's demand.

"We are at war with the frogs! Hold your bloody tongue, boy!"

"I am no mere boy, and you are not my father."

His lordship harrumphed and moved some papers around on his desk. "No, I'm not. But your father was a great man." A shadow passed over the older man's features. "He didn't deserve such an end."

"No one did," Etienne responded softly, his amusement dying a quick death. His father's demise at the hands of French revolutionaries remained an unpleasant and bitter memory.

His lordship leaned forward, the urgency and dissatisfaction in his expression telling Etienne how important the other man considered Sable's death.

"Sable must be stopped. Her latest kill had powerful relatives in the government."

Etienne shrugged one immaculately clad shoulder. He moved to the window, turning his back on the man who had taken him in so many years ago. "She has her own set of rules." Glancing down, he was surprised to see his fingers clenched. "Her rules for survival. What she's suffered..." He couldn't finish, his mind actually shying away from the barbarity of their lives.

"We can no longer support her activities. She must die."

Etienne turned to stare at his superior. "And that is all the reason I am to be given?"

Lord Castlereagh placed a small ornate jewel box in his hand. "Give this to her if you feel the need to soften the blow. It is time to end her suffering, du Clerc."

Fingers closing over the object, Etienne thought of the key secreted in his waistcoat pocket and sighed. "Yes, my lord."

**S**able stepped away from the pillar and disappeared, quickly becoming lost in warrens and alleys until she entered her own square. Her modest townhouse stood in one of the less fashionable parts of town. She was discreet so no one would note her comings and goings.

Sable's skirts rustled as she moved, French artistry in every line of her white muslin dress and outer wear. She clutched a penknife, one she'd removed from her fanciful, cherry-encrusted straw hat. It was an odd place to secret such an object, true, and quite perilous to her health should she slip. It could be extracted with ease, however, while pretending to adjust her headpiece.

As she entered her front parlor, her skin tingled. She wasn't alone. Turning, she forced a smile to stiff lips. "My dear Etienne. What brings you to my humble abode?"

He approached, bowing over her hand as he pressed his lips to her fingers. "A gentleman does not need a reason to call on so lovely a lady," he said smoothly, that hint of Paris in his tone.

Snatching back her appendage, she smothered her joyful response to his flattery in an unladylike grunt of disgust. "Such flattery is suspect, sir. Explain your presence or face the consequences."

She revealed her weapon, well aware that he knew she would use it.

His hands rose defensively. "There is no need for violence. Castlereagh did not send me."

"You come to release me from your loathsome possession?"

"No."

"Then get out. Or I will beat you and throw you out."

Etienne moved, his action so swift that she didn't see him until it was too late. He encircled her wrist with one strong hand, rendering her weapon useless. His other arm wrapped around her, trapping her free arm against her side.

Sable stared into his stormy blue eyes, her own narrowing in anger. He brought his face close, his lips a hairsbreadth away from hers. "Now, darling, do you want the neighbors gossiping about the Frenchies down the way? Our marriage is already too dramatic without the added titillation of supposition and falsehood."

Castlereagh didn't know he'd ordered Sable's husband to kill her.

Etienne slipped a fresh cravat around his neck and made short work of tying it. He glanced back at the young woman in the bed, her ebony tresses a startling contrast to the stark bed linens. Although her lips were swollen with his passionate kisses, her peaceful face resembled that of any other sleeping girl. One would never suspect her capable of such atrocities at her tender age.

A twinge of regret pierced him as she shifted, revealing a purple-blue mark on her wrist, bruised in their tussle beforehand. If only she would yield to his authority...

She stirred. "Etienne?"

"I am here," he murmured, his gaze traveling over her stunning features to the window beyond. "I leave presently. Night falls and you are expected to dine with Lady Jersey in—" he glanced at the mantle clock, "—one hour." He paused in the act of buttoning his waistcoat. "Can you be ready in time?"

"I will be," she said, her calm tone a warning that she lied.

He returned to the bed, kneeling on the feather ticking. He leaned over her, one hand on each side of her body, eyes hard and penetrating. "What are you planning, Sable?"

Her lips creased in a smug grin. "Nothing. I will be the most proper lady in attendance, I assure you."

"You lie."

"Quite often, husband, as do you. It is our trade."

He stared down at her, eyes narrowing with every long second that passed. Finally, he gave up, leaning down to kiss her hard, drawing a moan from her throat before releasing her abruptly.

She glared at him but remained cloaked in silence. Etienne knew he'd be called in to clean up another mess later.

With a sigh and a final tweak to his impeccable raiment, he said, "I must away. I will call for you tomorrow."

**S**he was weak.

Her dark eyes followed his heavily muscled form as he opened the door and disappeared. His confidence in her ready capitulation galled her. Dark blond hair, blue eyes, features chiseled from stone and the body of a Roman god—every young girl's dream prince, summoned to life from a childhood fantasy tale.

But the fairy tale ended with his appearance. Etienne was a scoundrel, a French nobleman who could lay claim to nothing more than a title and the clothes on his back. Like a well-trained hound, he followed every order his superiors gave him. His loyalties belonged not to Sable, but to France, Britain, and his twisted sense of morality. His fascination for her could no doubt be attributed to her *opposition* to France, Britain, and morality.

His legal ownership of her, sometimes referred to as marriage, meant nothing. His assignment to keep her under control made all the difference in their relationship. He cleaned up her messes and reported her activities to Castlereagh.

After her first meeting with Lord Castlereagh, she'd never seen his lordship again. Castlereagh had not seen the necessity, and she had seen no reason to argue.

A soft rage suffused her body. She rose, heedless of her nakedness, moving to ready herself for the coming night. A tiny slip of paper rested on her bedside table, the name of her next assignment scrawled inside. What a silly, yet unobtrusive way to inform her of her next mark.

Ignoring it, she moved to her dressing room, splashing her body with cold water. A maid would come in the morning, do the cleaning and cook the meals ahead of time, before returning home where she had a family of her own to care for. Meanwhile, Sable made do with what she could while alone.

And that was where Etienne had his uses. He helped when he was there, but he usually succeeded in seducing her as well—something that she both loved and hated in the same breath. Her independent nature rebelled against the confinement he represented, even if that meant security and love in the night.

She snatched the first gown from her clothespress and pulled it over her head, fastening the tapes. Often, ladies possessed a maid to help them dress, but Sable accomplished the difficult task on her own. She'd done for herself for many years.

She swiftly twisted her hair up and shoved several pins into place. Winding a string of flawless pearls into her black curls, she noticed the small box reflected in her mirror.

Turning her upper body, Sable stared at it. The small object peeked from behind a book, most of its form caught in shadow.

She knew that jewel case and the valuable item it protected. The case disappeared shortly after her parents' capture. Sable had avenged them, but the jewel case remained lost.

Her body rose as though a separate being, moving toward the small treasure in single-minded absorption. Fingers reached for and grasped the thing, a caress of adoration bestowed upon its shining black facade.

Who left it? Etienne? He was the logical choice. But when he had carried her into the room, she was already unaware of the tiny details, her mind caught up in the sensations her husband aroused.

She took up the spill of paper he'd left. A small item fell out, clattering on the table with a metallic click—her key without its chain.

The key that fit the case!

Unable to resist, she fit the key to the lock and turned it. Inside lay a beautiful pendant, stunningly wrought in aged silver and gold, a delicate silver chain pooled in the jewel case's bottom. Taking up the tiny pendant, her fingers brushed over its form, a small prayer box, its hinged lid sealed with wax.

A wave of nostalgia washed over Sable, tears filming her eyes. The box held every prayer her mother had whispered, every dream she'd dreamed and every longing in her heart. She had worn the pendant often, telling Sable that it held every good moment she'd ever known. And the little girl Sable had been such a short time ago believed the fantasy.

Working her fingernail beneath the box's lid, Sable broke the seal. A sickly sweet smell wafted over her, a familiar smell but one she did not experience often. The danger far outweighed the usefulness of the substance. Her vision blurring, she shook her head.

Panic set in and her fingers opened, releasing the pendant. Forcing her other hand to move, she took up the slip of paper and opened it.

Her husband's elegant script danced before her eyes. Just before they closed, her body crashed to the floor, the short message burning into her memory.

*I'm sorry.*

Étienne stared at her white face, a stark contrast to her upswept midnight tresses. Her clenched fingers still held his note, a silver pendant and a key close by.

A single tear escaped his eye, but he moved forward anyway. It was his job, after all, to clean up her messes.

# CROP CIRCLES
## Wendy Swore

*Sometimes you harvest more than crops.*

**H**oly crap." I stepped out of the waist high grain and onto the flattened area.

"You see it, Charley?" Uncle Joe trudged up from behind. The brittle wheat crunched beneath his boots as he came abreast.

"Yeah. It's just like you said—a genuine crop circle. I've seen them on TV, but this sure is something else—seeing it in person."

"You'll catch flies with your mouth hanging open like that—or is that the way you high school kids snag girls these days?" Joe guffawed at his own joke.

"Think it's real?"

"Naw. Ten bucks says it was them fool kids down the lane."

I tried to picture the neighbor kids making the crisp curved line forming the ring. Sure they were capable of smashing the wheat down—maybe on a dare or something—but this was done with machine precision. "Where are the footprints then?"

"The Sci-fi channel had a show once where people used boards to make the rings. Any fool could do it. Bet it took them all night. Look how big that other spot is over there. Dang kids."

"Can you save the wheat?" I knelt and threaded my fingers through the straw carpet to the moist soil beneath. Not only had the stalks been knocked down, but they'd been pressed into the dirt, the feathered heads crushed and the grains scattered. Could a couple of kids on some boards do that?

"No. It's ruined," said Uncle Joe.

A brown blur darted into the clearing a few yards from where I knelt—a field mouse. With a shrill squeak, it jerked like it'd been stung and zipped back under the cover of standing wheat. I watched it edge closer to the circle and stand on its hind legs, sniffing the air. After a moment, it ran off, skirting the rim around the side instead of crossing it.

Brushing my hands on my jeans, I accepted Uncle Joe's offered hand and stood. "Should we call the sheriff?"

"Naw, I got an idea." He leaned closer, a dirt encrusted finger tapping his temple. "I been thinking we might make out on this crop yet."

I glanced at the half dozen holes that dotted the field, like the ground opened up and swallowed the wheat whole. John Deere or otherwise, no combine on earth could fix this. "I don't see how. The wheat's ruined."

"We ain't going to harvest the wheat. See, the key is how you spin it. We call the news, let a reporter or two come with their cameras. How many people you think would come to see a bona fide alien circle?" He hooked his thumbs in the pocket of his bib-overalls and puckered his lips. "Yessir, I'd say three dollars a head oughta cover it, don't ya think?"

The first wave of reporters came early the next morning, and the waves just kept on coming. By the next week, guiding tourists to the circles was my full-time summer job. Uncle Joe set up a ticket booth by the entrance to the farm, and the fool kids from down the lane helped park the cars—though they wouldn't admit to making the circles.

Harvesting tourists is a lot easier than harvesting wheat, take the money, walk them to the first circle and keep watch so they don't go tramping through the rest of them. Easy money, until the tide changed and the waves ran out.

Uncle Joe was tickled pink as a prize hog at the fair. He bought a new hat and a pair of overalls, identical to his old pair, but with less dirt. In a fit of generosity, he bought me a pair of gloves and candy for the fool kids down the road. But his jovial mood didn't last. He'd taken to rocking on the porch with his mouth set in a grim line, his strong hands idle on his lap or rubbing his chin.

"Are you ready to harvest the wheat yet? We'll have to get it in soon or the frost will be here."

"Do you know we made more money in those three weeks than I make here in a year?"

"No, but hadn't we better—"

"Three weeks of sitting on my butt at the end of the lane, and I made enough to pay off the loan."

I waited to see where he was going with the thought, but he lapsed into silence and I left him to it. I couldn't fathom what sort of a mixed-up idea could keep a man sitting on his porch when a crop sat in the field ready to harvest.

A n early morning phone call had me stumbling out of the house and back over to Uncle Joe's place. His jubilant declaration nearly split my ears. "Hot dang, it happened again!"

But this time, when we stood at the edge of the clearing, I had a sneaking suspicion that the new circle wasn't a surprise. A red flush crept up his neck, and the vein in his head pounded out a rhythm something fierce. He dabbed his face with a kerchief.

"Well, I best call the reporters."

An odd crinkled pattern marred the floor of the clearing, which fell just shy of round. I narrowed my eyes at the boot-shaped depression several feet into the circle. The only alien that made this circle was a six-foot red-neck in bib-overalls.

I ran to the house to stop him, but my warnings fell on deaf ears.

"I told you! I woke up and saw it like that this morning. The news people liked it before, they'll like it again."

"But it isn't the same as before. You know it's not."

"Boy, you're worrying too much. There ain't nothing those fool kids can do that I can't do better." Joe deemed the pretense a necessary evil, a tiny nudge to get the tide of tourists rolling back again, but my gut twisted with worry over the deception.

Turns out, I was right to worry.

The cameras scanned the clearing for less than five minutes before the reporters turned their attention to Uncle Joe, and not long after that, the sheriff found him interesting too. I stood to the side, watching them lead him back to the cop car with the cameras flashing in his face and people firing off fast questions. Sweat rolled off his forehead.

"How do you feel about lying to the public about finding crop circles in your fields?"

"Do you belong to an alien cult?"

"Will you give refunds to the people who bought tickets?"

"How long did it take you to make the two new circles?"

Uncle Joe sputtered, "I didn't make two! I tell you I was set up. It's them fool kids down the lane. Someone should arrest them! Officer, I want to press charges!"

I ducked into the barn while the reporters zipped about snapping pictures, drawn to the scandal like bees to honey. After the last news van left, I walked back out to the field shaking my head. Momma had told me about some of Uncle Joe's hare-brained ideas when they were kids, but she would drop a calf over this one.

I walked through the crop circle that wasn't and paused by the far side. Didn't they say something about two new circles? Sure enough, not twenty paces ahead, another perfect hole had been cut out of the field.

"Now how in the world did he manage to do that?" My fingers brushed the wheat heads as I approached the new spot. The uniform lay of the wheat, the perfect slice at the edge, made it hard to believe that the same man had done them both. If it really was the fool kids, then they did a fine job.

"How on earth did he do it? Why would this circle be perfect and the other such a mess?"

Light rippled out from the center of the clearing and radiated outward like rays on a dial. I stumbled back and fell on my rear. My heart thudded with adrenaline so hard that I half expected it to go galloping across the field on its own.

A brilliant light split the air before me, and a doorway appeared hovering in midair several feet off the ground. My mind screamed for me to run, but it got lost in the translation and my body sat where I'd fallen and shook like a leaf. I couldn't take my eyes off the door, and the figure who occupied it.

Grotesquely large, the head wobbled on the neck as if one strong gust of wind might send it rolling off across the field. Grey skin coated its body, and the feet seemed to hover just off the floor. It raised its three-fingered hand.

My mouth opened and shut like a fish. An alien! A real honest-to-goodness alien. I meant to say something like "what do you want?" But my tongue got all kerfluffed and all that popped out was "how."

"How do we make the circles? Easy." The alien pointed to the ship around him. "The key is how you spin it."

# SYMBIOTE
## Rita J. Webb

*Programmed to serve for life,*
*how can a slave girl break away?*

Standing on the highest roof in the city, I leaned over the side and peered down. Far below me, clouds swallowed up the lights and noises of the city. My hands clenched, nails digging into my palms, tears streaming down my face. Lost. Alone. Empty. I felt as if the world had devoured me and left me to die.

The sky above stretched like an open canvas. Stars glistened and twinkled as though they spoke to each other in some secret language. If only I could decipher the stars' code, maybe they would transport me to their magical world—a place of *freedom*.

But my heart was too black and broken to understand them.

*"You do this every day, RW1211. Why do you not fly there?"* The metallic voice tinkled in my head. I hated that voice, and yet I cherished it. My secret. My only friend.

Maybe I wasn't the latest model of cybernetic organisms, just a malformed cripple with a computer box mounted to my back, an awkward girl—not yet a woman—a hopeless reject. But my engineers hadn't designed me to hear voices from thin air. Perhaps I had gone mad or a virus corrupted the chip in my brain. Or maybe years of human contact gave my symbiotic parts a human quality, a pretended sentience. No matter the cause, if my department's managers learned of this, they would retire me.

"I'm too young to be retired."

*"If you keep doing this, you will get caught."*

"Hush. You're ruining the moment."

*"Moments cannot be ruined."*

"Well, you're ruining mine."

*"People do not own moments."*

I ignored the voice and sighed. Out here, above the city, the air was fresh. A crisp wind blew over me; the tiny hairs on my arm stirred in the breeze. Bumps formed in tantalizing rows across my skin. I closed my eyes and spread my arms wide, throwing my head back. I spun in a circle. *Alive. I'm alive.*

*I'm alive and you can't take that from me.*

I squeezed my eyes shut. My heart burned in my chest. I spun faster.

*"Stop. You make me dizzy."*

"You can't get dizzy. You're a machine."

*"No, I am alive. Just like you."*

"You're a bucket of bolts, and talking like that will get us both killed."

*"I have dreams."*

"Running through your stored images during stasis isn't dreaming. You're such a child."

*"Children are alive, so I must be alive too."*

"Fine, you're alive. Just shut up about it already."

How a computer could simulate sulking, I had no idea.

A click sounded at the roof's door, and my heart stopped. I darted behind the air-cooling machines, ducking as the door swung open. My breath came out in short, ragged bursts.

Footsteps clicked across the roof. I counted each sound of the heels against the concrete, picturing the figure passing by the chicken coop, the gardens, the first cooling unit. I bit my lip to stifle my gasp. Any moment, the stranger would step around the corner and see me.

Another step.

Panicked, I stumbled backward, landing with a thud against the solar panels behind me.

"I heard you. Might as well come out now. Making me search for you will only—"

"I'm sorry. I was only looking at the stars." I stepped out, my head bowed. Writhing worms of fear squirmed in my stomach.

"That is forbidden. You know the laws."

"I won't do it again. I promise."

My hands shook. I swallowed the lump in my throat—guilt that burned its way down my chest and then churned in the acid of my stomach. The company clothed me, fed me, and gave me a warm place to sleep. When my parents couldn't keep me, the company became my mother and my father. My family. They changed me into something useful—a machine smart enough to program intricate algorithms, strong enough to endure fourteen hours of labor in one stretch, and yet I still had the intuition only a human can fathom.

And now I betrayed them by wishing for something else, for a nameless feeling I didn't understand.

I glanced up. The guard folded his arms and looked down his nose. Blue eyes hammered into me, reminding me of every rule I ever broke. I tried to look away, but his cold stare held mine. With trembling fingers, I pushed back my frizzy red hair. Cropped in the required fashion, it stayed behind my ear barely a moment before it slipped back out and tickled my face.

"Name and department."

"Sorry." Wincing, I pushed my arm forward and looked away.

*"Never been caught before. This will go on your permanent record."*

*Don't be so amused.*

"Name and department."

He had the scanner in hand; he could read the barcode on my arm and know everything about me since I first came here at the ripe old age of five. Everything except my real name and whatever it was that drove me up here in the darkest hour of the night.

He could turn me in, and I'd be screwed. But he didn't move.

"RW1211 from Robotic Inventions for Transformation Automation," I whispered.

"I have to report this, you know."

"Please. Any—anything you want." I glanced away, embarrassed.

He snorted. "Anything? What do you take me for?"

I glared up at him.

"Feisty." His eyes twinkled, reminding me of the stars. His black curls danced with his silent laughter, mocking me.

"Maybe I came up here *once* to stare at the stars, but that doesn't mean I've betrayed the Company. I still do my job."

*"Once?"*

No, not once. Many times. And every time, I promised myself never again. I felt sick for my weakness. But days later, sweating, shaking with this strange need, I found myself sneaking through the corridors, hiding from cameras and guards, and carefully unbolting the locked door without triggering the alarm—as if my desire for the stars was some kind of drug.

"That's not what I meant. You know the rules: No breeding outside your department."

My ears burned. "I didn't say—"

"Yes, you did."

Hands clenched, I opened my mouth and then snapped it back shut. He laughed at me like the devil had told him a dirty joke. I wanted to slap him or shake him, but to do so meant spending a day in the sensory-deprivation tanks.

"Look, you're *almost* pretty. Not my type, but that red hair of yours is rather fetching, even with a stubby nose and freckles. I'll let you go this time, but if I catch you again..."

I stared at him wordlessly, pressing my lips together, wishing my eyes could set him on fire. Try as I might, I could think of nothing to say to wipe the smug look off his face. Still laughing, he took my shoulders, turned me about, and pushed me back through the door.

Chin up, back straight, I marched down the stairs toward my quarters. I felt his eyes watching me, crawling on my skin like burning fingers.

*"You will be back in a week."*

"No, not this time. I swear it."

*"Addictions are hard to break."*

The noise of static reminded me of laughter.

The morning alarm chimed, pulling me from an ocean of dreams where a happy oblivion relieved me from the drudgery that is my life. I groaned, stretched, and yawned, peeking out at the world through the slit of my eyes. The lights sliced into me. Pushing my blankets away before they could entice me to roll over and go back to sleep, I sat up.

My eyes snapped open, and I shivered, bare skin bristling from the cold. A fresh jumpsuit hung where I had left the last one. With no clothes of my own, I wore the same green one-size-fits-all outfit, issued to the entire department. Pushing my feet inside, I pulled it on and adjusted the straps giving me some customization—loose fitting clothes weren't safe around the machinery.

Printed on the shoulder, the company name— *Emerson Dixon Industries Technology*—appeared next to a key-shaped logo, matching the tattoo above my barcode. One of the best companies in the industry owned me. The other units in my department wore their marks with pride. But I figured it didn't matter who owned me; I wasn't free.

BL1105, a tiny girl with big blue eyes, sat down beside me and gave me a conspiratorial wink. She loved to discover everybody's secrets, and her curiosity scared my frizzy hair straight. I learned long ago to avoid her.

"So where did you go last night? Did you finally accept *his* invitation? FP0912 is rather cute. You should give him a chance."

*"The security guard was cuter."*

Hard to admit, but the computer was right. Maybe FP was the boy assigned to me, but his lack of chin made him look like a snake, and his breath smelled of spoiled milk. The idea of his hands on me made my stomach churn.

I glanced around. Workers, male and female, half naked, spilled out of bunks, zipped into their jumpsuits, and shuffled toward the public restroom. A metal box protruded from their backs, a bulky lump under their green jumpsuits. Nobody gave me a second glance, their eyes bright and focused, ready to face the day. Ready to serve. *Sheeple.*

Was I the only one who wished for something more?

*"Thinking of their duties, no doubt. Unlike you."*

"Sure, rub it in," I mumbled.

"What was that?" BL asked.

"Um, nothing. I just got up to go to the bathroom, is all."

"Bull."

"Did to."

She put her arm around my shoulders. I resisted the urge to shrink away. "You know I have your best interests at heart, sweetie. You have to get your act together. You're up for review soon, and if they knew…"

She patted my head in that big-sister-knows-everything fashion. I sighed, tuning her out. Word for word, the rest of the lecture would go as it always did. Our duty was to serve and obey; the company fed us, clothed us, and housed us; I would miss my advancement; I might get retired early in disgrace; my future depended on following the rules; I needed to be a team player; staring at the stars was a foolish waste of time...

"Don't make waves—"

*"Be a three. Mediocre."*

"I know. I know. 'You have to think about the company.'"

"You got it. Come on; let's get breakfast." BL clapped me on the back and grinned.

Was this really all there was to life?

As it was against the rules to talk during mealtime, silence rang through the cafeteria. I lined up with the others to trudge through the breakfast line. You ate what they served—a bowl of lumpy oatmeal, a piece of dried out sausage, a bruised banana, and a carton of skim milk. Your only choice—sugar or plain. But they recorded every spoonful, and later, they would make you pay. Selecting something special for yourself was frowned upon.

Not much of a choice.

Color-coded tables filled the room. All around me, people ate methodically—little robots, doing what they were told. I hated the neat little rows of automatons, in their stiff uniforms, cold faces with empty eyes. Thinking of twinkling stars and sparkling blue eyes, I moved to the green zone and sat down next to BL1105. Moving spoon to mouth mechanically, I ate my porridge like the empty shell I pretended to be.

BL nudged my elbow. I looked up to see my manager MX0409 standing across the table, shooting daggers from her eyes. In place of a jumpsuit, she wore a green pantsuit, clean, crisp, and annoyingly perfect; her brown hair had been plastered to her head, not one strand out of place. She had arrived here the same time I had, and for a while, we were friends. But then they brainwashed her, and duty has no place for friendship.

Beside her stood my project lead, KG0923, a triumphant sneer stuck to his face like dried egg. I avoided his eyes so he wouldn't see the rebellion and hatred I couldn't hide.

Incompetent KG couldn't plan the procedures if I'd printed all the answers in bold and hand-fed it into his data drive, and everyone knew it. But he could kiss their collective golden butts to satisfaction. Somehow, he could make doing nothing all day sound as if the entire department depended on him. Where competency failed, ardor reigned.

He hated me for making him look bad with my careful precision and attention to detail. For the rest of my life, he would make me pay for it.

"You reprogrammed the service options against test protocol." MX's voice rang out over the din of spoons hitting bowls, chairs sliding, and trays slapping tables. Every eye in the room burned against my cold skin.

"The current options didn't apply to the matrix; I had to—"

She cocked an eyebrow at me, and I snapped my mouth shut. I felt sick. I had disobeyed the rules. Again.

"KG0923 has seniority on this project. You will remove your changes as soon as breakfast is over, and after your standard twelve hours, you will report to my office."

*Joy. Kitchen duty.*

*"If we're lucky."*

M eeting is in session." The Man stared at each person at the table in turn. Standing on a pedestal, his five-foot frame towered over the collection of gray suits. His knuckles pressed against the rich mahogany surface; his beady eyes leered at the members of the board through his thick glasses.

Nobody dared to meet his gaze. Nobody dared to look away either. Instead they looked past his shoulder or stared at his pale forehead or studied the fat mustache gracing his lip.

The Man sat down in a golden chair with velvet cushions and leaned back. A servant put a glass in his hand, ice rattled in the brown elixir. The room shifted uncomfortably as ten pairs of eyes watched the Man sip his drink.

"Director of Finance, give me the report I requested on current employee costs."

The financier's suit matched his gray face, blank gray eyes, and the gray hair peppering the black fur bristling on the top of his head. He focused his eyes on the wall ahead of him and spoke in a gray monotone, "Maintenance on the early cybernetic models has doubled in the past year. An extraordinary amount of money is spent on keeping their networks from shutting down. With the newer models, we will strategically maneuver toward the cutting-edge innovations, putting us ahead of our competitors and placing us at the forefront of our industry.

"Now these charts show the cost of current repairs, the purchase of new replacement models, and the cost of housing and caring for retired employees—"

Collective gasps and cries of horror rose around the table.

"An outrage!"

"Ten years of labor does not entitle them to millions of our hard-earned profits."

"The company cannot afford to be strapped down by that kind of burden."

The Man leaned back in his chair and smiled as his board of advisors responded, their faces animated with pretend emotion. They were the choir and he, the gifted director; they were the crew and he, the captain of this ship, driving it ever onward to greater glory. He was Caesar. He was Napoleon.

He was their god.

"Director."

The room quieted. All eyes turned to the Man on the throne.

"They would no longer be employees if they retired. We are not a charity. Get your priorities straight."

Face as gray and emotionless as when he started, the financial director nodded slowly and sat back down.

The Man ran his hand down the paper before him. "Director of Human Resources."

A woman shuffled her papers; the sound jarred the silence in the room. She cringed, stood, and cleared her throat, her ebony skin glistening, gray suit clinging to her sweaty skin. Shaking hands pushed her hair away from her eyes. "Legally, we are required to provide retired employees a cozy settlement, but if we can document a performance decline, we can—can recycle them."

"Good. Continue."

"This paper details the requirements. This will be a phased effort, starting with reprimands and finally ending with poor performance reviews. After a year, we can file the petition with the Congressional Committee for Stressed Corporations—"

"A year, madam?"

"W-we can forge them, Sir."

"That's better."

She looked down and folded her hands on her lap. The stacks of paper before her angled crookedly, and she straightened the corners so not one lay out of place, as if perfection and precision could blot out her mistakes.

"Director of Operations, what have you to say?"

Another man stood. He fidgeted with the gray cuffs of his suit, plucking at imaginary lint, and pulled at his tight collar; his mouth opened and closed like a fish trying to suck water out of the dry air. He looked about at the empty eyes staring at him.

"The Generation F models continue to produce at a higher pace than any other model on our—"

"Not what I want to hear."

"Our production rates will falter, and the new COGS—"

"Which stands for...?"

"Cybernetic Organisms Generation S will never be able to replace the Generation F model in competency and performance. Although their programming and technology is more advanced, testing has shown certain defects in their cognitive and adaptive skills." He rushed through his words, ignoring the interruptions. Two red marks formed on his pale face, and when he finished speaking, he panted as though he had raced through all one hundred fifty flights of stairs to reach the conference room at the top of the building.

"There will be nothing wrong with their performance. They will work as I expect, or I will find someone else to direct them."

Red spots faded, and the Operations Director swallowed.

"Well?"

"No, Sir."

"No?"

"Yes. Sir."

"Good. Work with Human Resources to meet the legal documentation."

**N**obody knew an entity listened over the phone system, shaking its virtual head sadly.

TJ0120 leaned against the wall in the abandoned, darkened hallway. A door stood open to an old conference room, and inside was his mentor, one of the directors, but which, TJ had no clue. All he knew was that this man wanted to help people escape and had the means to make it happen. Until now no one had successfully made it out. TJ vowed he would be the first.

"Your key code?" The hoarse voice came through the open door.

"V-X14387." His heart raced as silence met his words. Whoever stood on the other side of this wall would be validating his credentials, verifying who he was in the organization, what he did, and if he really was part of the resistance. If found unworthy, he would be dead before the man—or woman—had given him any indication he had failed to pass inspection.

"Proceed."

TJ took a deep breath. "I found a candidate for the program."

"Who?" The scraggly voice came through the open door.

"A woman, not much more than a girl. But she's got that look in her eyes."

"Department?"

"Robotic Inventions for Transformation Automation."

"Yes, the R.I.T.A. program. They are on the list for termination."

"Retirement?" TJ crossed his fingers.

"Recycling."

*Followed by incineration, no doubt.*

Not good news. That would leave little time. His mind whirled through the possibilities, discarding them as quickly as he found them.

"You have the money cards ready and the location of a safe house?"

"Yes."

"Good. Permission granted."

TJ's shoulders slumped, relief flooding through him. He looked about, to make sure no one watched him from the shadows, and skulked down the hall. Fear, excitement, and turmoil tumbled through him. He would take the step he'd waited for. But would he survive?

I filed into the conference room, white walls, glaring lights, and neat rows of white, plastic chairs. The noises of shuffling feet and scraping chair legs on the white tile floor reverberated about the room.

Our manager, her crisp green suit rustling as she moved, handed out green folders to each of us. We filled up the seats, starting with row one, seat one, until every available chair was taken. Forty employees, forty seats, forty folders. Leaning forward to make room for the cold protrusion on our backs, we craned our necks to see the front of the room.

A man with a gray suit stood at a podium. His sunken cheeks looked like rubber, and his eyes stared straight ahead as if dull, gray rocks had been stuck in his sockets. The light didn't even reflect in them.

"It is with great honor that I announce your department's promotion to operational advisors. New cyborgs will replace your position, ten for each one of you. And your job will be to see that they function in their new roles. Open your packets to page one. I will go over each detail. Hold all questions until the end."

His sodden monotone made my eyelids droop dangerously low; I pinched my leg to stay awake and opened my folder. I was a good little slave girl, after all. Printed across the top, my name *RW1211* stood out in bold letters, and below it, a note, handwritten in block letters, stuck to the page with a bit of tape.

*"Oh, a note. How nice. Perhaps if we set it on end, it will dance for us."*

"Shut up," I whispered hoarsely. People turned to glare at me, lips pressed together, brows furrowed. *Oops.* I gave an apologetic smile. They huffed. My face burned, and I ducked my head back into my green folder.

The note read:

*If you want to escape, meet me on the roof at the beginning of the new cycle.*

Blood roared in my ears; my vision blurred. This couldn't be real. A trap. A trap. It had to be a trap. Had the security guard turned me in anyway? I hadn't broken my promise!

"In your new role, you will each be given your own sleeping quarters in the upper floors of the tower. You will have access to a recreation room, a swimming pool, an exercise facility—anything you could possibly want. If you turn to page two, you will see pictures of the available retirement facilities."

*"Sure, they'll give you anything but the stars."*

The sound of paper swishing filled the room. The next page displayed smiling faces, shining with happiness; some enjoyed drinks at a small table, others toweled off at the poolside.

"Now if you turn to the next page, you will find the countdown to your retirement day. There will be a six month knowledge transfer period as the new models learn to take over your positions. This will be a smooth process in which the new COGS models work alongside you. Six months from now, you will have a life of ease."

*"If they don't kill you first..."*

"Don't be silly," I murmured, as quiet as a whisper of air. No one looked at me. No one even stirred, so entranced in the speech. A few nodded their heads. Others had mouths hanging open; drool should have been running down their chins.

*"I am a computer. I am never silly."*

I snorted. Nobody except the man at the front noticed. His eyes narrowed.

*"I am a computer. I can go anywhere there is an electrical line and an electronic device. You really should learn to listen to me more."*

**I** don't know why I came."

*"You know why. Oh look, a bird. I think it is a nightingale."*

There was no bird. Just a breeze and the humming of the air conditioning units.

I stared up at the stars too far away to touch. I shook my fist at them, a tear slipped down my face. Damn the stars. Damn freedom and dreams. Damn the promises those dreams whispered to me night after night, drawing me back here to stare at twinkling stars.

I kicked the chicken coop; the hens squawked. I picked up stones and threw them at the air conditioning units. They hit with a ping and then rolled away with a thud against the roof wall. Looking around for something else to punch, I found nothing else but a garden and some solar panels. Instead, I swung at the empty air.

"They'll kill me if whoever left the note turns me in."

*"They will do that anyway."*

They promised me a life of ease, but here I stood. Throwing away my future.

What was wrong with me?

*"If you didn't come, you will always wonder. Could I have been telling the truth? That is, until they recycle you. Then for a brief moment, you will regret not listening to me."*

The door swung open, creaking. My hands shook; I pressed them to my sides to stop the trembling. But I lifted my chin and faced the man as he stepped out. The same guard from before, the same cocky grin, the same silky, black curls.

"You!" I stomped my foot and pointed at him, ready to give him a piece of my mind.

He put his finger to his mouth; his eyes darted about the rooftop. I followed his gaze, searching the shadows, but nothing was there. Then he studied my face—my eyes, my mouth—and then ran his hands over my head, behind my ears, along my body, tracing the box at my back.

*How dare he?* "I'm. Not. Wired!"

"I hoped you would come. Hurry; we don't have much time."

He grabbed my hand, and before I could protest, we flew down the metal stairs that spiraled into the belly of a one-hundred-twenty-story beast. Our feet clanged and echoed throughout the concrete chamber, leading down into a dark pit, tracing back down the same stairs I had climbed to find escape.

"Wait. Where are we going?"

"No time. I'll explain later."

Should I stop him, make him explain himself? But my feet kept moving as if they had a will of their own. As if some force—destiny maybe—had swept me up. Halfway down, we entered a deserted hall; painting rags, buckets, brushes were strewn around the floor. The lighting was dim, and I had to pick my way carefully.

A heavy metal door with a key pad and a hand scanner blocked the end of the hall. Standing four feet high and four feet wide, it looked more like a cupboard set into the wall. He typed a code *V-X14387*, slipped a latex glove over his hand, and pressed it to the scanner. I held my hand over my heart to keep it from beating out of my chest and looked back.

"Where are we?" I whispered.

"Shush."

He didn't even look at me, glancing back up the empty hall. The door slid open with a mechanical hum, and we crawled into utter blackness, the door swinging shut behind me. Below and to the sides of me, the smooth surface rounded into a small passageway. I felt my way blindly, inch by inch.

The nasty stench of rancid meat filled the air. I gagged and choked, trying to cover my face with the collar of my jumpsuit.

*"Do you smell that? That's the smell of freedom."*

Then suddenly I plunged forward. Sliding. Falling.

Falling. Screaming.

His laughter rose up from below me.

*I'm going to die.*

*"Stop screaming. You sound ridiculous."*

I shut my mouth. I closed my eyes, imagining the stars had finally snatched me away. Floating ever downward, spiraling. The direction of the chute changed, and our freefall slowed until we stopped. I opened my eyes. Trash piled all around us, and above lay the open sky.

"Now was that so bad?" He smiled at me. His teeth dazzled and sparkled.

"Am I—am I free?"

"Not yet, but if we run fast enough, we can get out of here before they find us." With a grunt, he rolled over and pushed himself up. He grabbed my hand and pulled me up with him.

Once again, he dragged me forward, slipping and sliding across piles of debris. When we got to the dirty metal wall, he pushed me up and then climbed beside me. He jumped down onto the open road. "Come on. I'll catch you."

"I'll fall."

"*Either risk the fall or stay here for them to find us. Your choice.*"

I jumped.

With a grunt, he caught me. "Was that so bad?"

"No."

"Let's go." He took my hand and turned away from the building complex that had been my home all of my life.

I didn't run. I flew. My limbs felt light. Clouds carried me.

Street lights led us through the quiet city. I threw my head back and laughed.

*Freedom.*

# WHERE THEY BELONG
## Paige Ray

*Ever feel like you don't belong?*
*Maybe you don't.*

standing at the curb, Clara's gaze followed the blue station wagon that pulled into the school parking lot to pick her up.

"Clara! Wait!"

Students poured from the high school, sunlight splattering their faces. Clara scanned the milling crowd, scurrying off to cars or loading onto buses. In the midst of it all, her eyes found her friend Camber who ran toward her, waving, a grin plastered on her freckled face.

Clara smiled. "Another note?"

"My last one."

"Camber! Come on! We're going to be late for the movie!" Kate bellowed from her car. Camber handed Clara the note and scurried toward the parking lot.

"See you Monday," Clara called.

The blue banana wagon pulled to the curb and rattled to a stop. Clara climbed in and kissed the soft, wrinkled cheek of her grandmother. "Oh Nana, I had a great day. I got an A on my Biology test."

"That's my girl."

They headed toward the crime-riddled street and the dinky little house they lived in. Clara, her grandmother, her mother, and her little sister.

"How are you today?"

"I'm good, dear. What'd yer friend want?" she asked in her strong Oklahoma accent.

"Oh, that was Camber; she just wanted to give me this note. We also got to dissect a shark today," Clara replied, knowing it would get a reaction from her grandmother.

"Oh gawd, that sounds nasty. Good job on your test though."

"Thanks..." Clara opened the note.

Dear Clara,

Please don't take this the wrong way. We all think you're alright.

Here's the deal though, you aren't like us. You live in a bad area and we all live in Grenadine Knolls.

That's the first problem—you're poor. You can never afford to do anything with us.

The other thing is that you are weird. It's almost like you weren't meant to be human, or at least on this planet.

So, we wanted to let you know that you can't hang out with us anymore. It doesn't match up.

We are truly sorry things are this way, but you do understand. You're smart, so we are sure you do.

Good luck finding friends you actually fit in with.

See you around.

Lara Kate Camber Eliza

P.S. Please don't call any of us with pathetic pleading. It will only make it worse for you. Have a great weekend.

That evening, Clara read the letter while sitting in her garage, the only place she could be alone. She opened the paper, damp with her tears, for the thousandth time.

"Why?" she said to no one in particular.

The girls treated her nice enough all year, except for the occasional sneer when she couldn't go where they wanted to go. Their parents gave them everything they wanted and half the time they claimed to hate their parents. At least they still had both parents. Clara thought about her father that had left her family only a few years earlier with debts and broken promises.

She wiped the last few tears from her face and swallowed hard. Lifting her chin and pressing her lips together in a firm white line, she swore there would be no more tears.

"Mom, you still want to go for our walk?" she asked as her mother came out to start a load of laundry. They sometimes visited a nearby trail adorned with trees and benches. There, she could clear her mind, or think in tune with her body as she so often did—both methods would probably help her right about now.

"Sure honey, are you going to be okay?" Worry lines creased her mother's forehead. Searching her eyes, her mother tucked a stray strand of auburn hair behind her daughter's ear. Clara swallowed the lump in her throat; she needed to be tough.

"Yeah, Mom, I'm fine...I will be fine. Not the kind of people I would want to be around anyway with notes like this." She waved the note in the air, then tore it up into little pieces and tossed it in the trash can.

"Yeah, honey, people like that don't deserve your company anyway."

Clara wiped one more tear away, aware of her mother watching. Her mom's face looked thin, framed by hair streaked with gray. Dark rings shadowed her eyes. Clara wished she could wipe away all of the worries and pain.

"Okay, I'll put on my shoes." She ran to get her battered tennis shoes.

When they got to the cliffs, the warm orange sunset kissed Clara's skin. A light breeze blew through her hair, and the sound of the wild river crashed against the rocks below. Excitement sent an electric tingle through her body.

She jumped out of the car as they parked and stumbled over the sidewalk. Her mom had parked close to the cliff's edge, and Clara rolled, about to fall over the cliff's edge. She reached for anything to stop her slide, grabbing a large rock beside the trail.

As she caught her breath, bracing herself so she wouldn't fall, Clara caught a glint of something shiny hidden beneath the rock on the wall of the cliff. She reached, gritting her teeth in concentration and grasped it with the tips of her fingers. A silver key. Time and the elements had created a partial barrier, encasing it in a crusty black substance smelling like a mixture of cleaning supplies.

Clara climbed back onto the cliff as her mom got to her.

"Oh dear, are you okay?" Clara shoved the key into her pocket.

"Do we need to take you to the hospital? Are you hurt? Did you hit your head? Are there any broken bones?" Her mom hugged her tightly before precise hands explored Clara's head and arms, looking for injuries. A look of panic filled her eyes, but she still held a somewhat calm demeanor.

"I'm fine, mom. I was a little excited and then stumbled over the sidewalk. I'm fine; let's go."

"You sure?"

Clara rolled her eyes. "Yeah, just want to walk this day off."

The key, now cleaned and placed beneath her hand-me-down pillow, found its way into her dreams, whispering secrets to her. It told Clara that she was *meant* to find it; someone had put the key there, for her. The whispers suggested that the key belonged to a long line of super humans, not super-heroes, just humans who were a little extra. *Special.*

Key in hand, Clara walked through the halls of her school, all the way to the Auditorium, the oldest building on campus. Behind the stage stood a door. Since the wall was so thin, it didn't appear to open to anywhere. Clara inserted her silver key into the lock and turned it. She reached for the knob—

BEEP! BEEP! BEEP! BEEP!

Clara groaned. Right in the middle of one of the most mysterious, yet exciting dreams of her life, and it was time to get ready for another Monday morning.

"Clara, get up and get ready. You don't want to be late," Nana said from across the room. Clara shared a room with her grandmother while her little sister, Anna, shared a room with their mother.

After showering and drying her hair, she wondered if she *would* be late with only thirty minutes left to eat her breakfast and walk to school. She almost always ran late, too caught up in her own mind to pay much attention to time.

"We get to play dodge ball today at school. I'm going to win," Anna spouted over her bowl of cereal.

"I bet you will win too, Sis." Clara rumpled her little sister's still unfixed hair. She gathered her backpack and took off out the door. She would have to keep a fast pace if she wanted to get to school on time.

"Hi, Clara. I thought you would need someone to walk with today, so here I am." Sorin, her friend who lived in the trailer park around the corner, beamed at her from the sidewalk. Maybe not the best looking, but he was a very sweet boy, and someone Clara considered a friend. And like her, he didn't fit in at school either. His strange obsession with science fiction books and obscure poetry may have been the catalyst for that reputation.

"Sure, Sorin. We have to walk fast though. It's already late."

"I know; I can keep up."

Silence hung heavy on the way to school, punctuated by Sorin's high-pitched laughter at her occasional lame jokes. He had the nice-guy routine down pat, though he wasn't really her type. But sometimes, she felt a spark of interest for him, how his smile would warm her thoughts and her blood. Though, she was sure that she didn't want to ruin their friendship.

"See you later, Clara. Have a great day." Sorin winked as he went off to his first class. Clara felt her breath catch.

"We'll see about that," Clara muttered under her breath as she walked to class. She shoved her hand in her pocket and realized she had forgotten the key. Crappers! She couldn't go back home now. She would have to wait until the next day to explore the mysterious door.

She sat down at her desk for the first class. Unfortunately, she shared this class with Lara. Lara looked at her with a snide expression and smiled a devilish grin that spread like wildfire across her rosy cheeks. It made Clara want to puke.

If only people knew who Lara crushed over and how she had humiliated herself confessing her love for him, promising she would do anything for him, to him, whenever he wanted and then cried for hours on Clara's shoulder when he laughed and rejected her. That would teach her a thing or two.

A nice fantasy, but no, Clara refused to stoop to their level.

A few classes later, she shared a class with Kate, who glared with a look like an old witch. Maybe spreading a rumor about all of the boyfriends would serve her right...but the boyfriends were just an attempt to fill the void of her absentee parents who were always on vacation. Poor girl, Clara actually felt sorry for her.

By lunchtime, Clara's heart felt lighter, only sad she had forgotten her key; this would have been the time to try it out. She quietly ate her school lunch, turkey and gravy with mashed potatoes formed with an ice cream scooper when Sorin sat down across from her.

"Hey Clara-Bell, how's it going? Are you going to eat that?" Using his stupid pet name for her, he pointed at the vomit-like mass called peach cobbler.

"No, you can have it. You like to eat more than me."

"What can I say? I'm a growing boy with a hollow leg."

Clara smiled. Sorin made her happier than most things in her life. A sense of warmth ran through her veins, a feeling she had never known before.

They would have their next class together, so Sorin ate his lunch while Clara contemplated the new feeling that Sorin washed over her. She kept staring at Sorin's dark blue eyes.

"What?" he asked, smiling like a goof. She quickly snapped out of it and looked down at her plate. The bell rang.

"Uh…nothing, just thinking. I'm going to use the restroom, meet you in class." Clara bounded toward the restroom. As she rushed off, she could hear Sorin say something, but couldn't make it out with all of the chatter in the cafeteria. She glanced behind her. The fool grinned, the biggest grin she had ever seen. Turning back around, she smiled too and ran right into the door. How embarrassing. She could hear Sorin's laughter behind her as she scurried through the offending door, her cheeks a blazing hot red.

Clara stepped into the restroom. In front of the mirror, fixing her lip gloss, stood Eliza. Clara could feel the heat on her face. Keeping her eyes down, she walked toward the stalls.

"Clara?" Eliza turned away from the mirror and came closer.

"Yeah?" Clara kept her eyes down, pretending disinterest.

"Please listen to me; I didn't want to write that note. I only wrote a few lines, you know my handwriting. I don't feel that way at all. I think you're a great person, but I can't give them up as friends. Please forgive me. I couldn't stand being alone. You seem to do it alright." Eliza looked like she might cry. Clara sucked in a breath; now was her chance to get back in her way.

"Eliza, I will be fine. Thank you for telling me. I appreciate your honesty. Now, I have to pee; go run off to your little friends." Clara smiled the condescending grin that her mother always lectured her for using.

Eliza didn't realize and smiled back. She bounced out of the door. Sheltered in a bubble world by her parents, Eliza was stuck in baby mode. She talked like a baby and had no clue what real life was like. How sad for her. If everyone knew she still played with Barbies, the teasing would never stop.

Nah, still not feeling like their level.

By the last class of the day, band, Clara felt great. Unfortunately, she shared that class with Kate. How could she get away from these brats? Clara turned to hear Kate and a new unsuspecting victim whispering and snickering in the row behind her. She snorted—as if those silly trumpet players could bother her! Playing first chair flute music was one of her few joys in life.

Grinning like a silly monkey, she turned her back on them, focusing on the sheet of music in front of her. She held her head high, chin firm, and refused to let them see any weakness.

As the class put away their instruments and headed out the doors, Kate stopped her. "You seem to be doing fine." Her voice sounded bewildered, and wide as tractor tires, her eyes stood out on her face.

"Sure am." Clara walked out of the room. Thinking of the shock on Kate's face, she chuckled.

T hat night, Clara dreamt of the key again, but this time the door swung open on creaky hinges. Sorin trembled beside her.

"Where are we going, Clara-Bell?"

"I don't know."

"Please, hold my hand; I'm a little scared."

"Okay, come on," she pushed the door open.

An old hallway headed toward the back of the auditorium, strewn with dusty spider webs and old velvet carpet. The musty, damp smell burned her nose.

They went down the slim corridor to another door at the far end. Her blood raced through her veins, and her breath came in little gasps. When Clara reached for the door, the familiar beep of her alarm dragged her back to reality.

Before anything else, she grabbed the key from under her pillow and stuffed it into the pocket of her jeans lying on the bathroom counter.

"I won't forget you today, little buddy."

Same routine as always, she headed to school with Sorin, rushing because they were late, only slowing down as the school came in sight.

"Sorin, meet me before lunch. I have something to show you."

"Okay, I'll be there." Sorin ran off to his first class, with a smile plastered on his face.

At lunchtime, she grabbed Sorin's sleeve in one hand and the key in the other and led them to the crumbling Auditorium. She then proceeded to drag them behind the curtain at the back of the stage.

"So, what are you going to show me, Clara?" He fidgeted and cleared his throat.

"This." Clara pulled out the key. It seemed to glow now that it was closer to the mysterious door.

"A key?"

"Not just any key; the key to *this* door." She pointed at the rotting door, the wooden boards gray with age. A rusted knocker took up the top half.

"We're going in there? There can't be a room beyond this door. The wall's too thin!"

"I saw this key open that door."

"How did you see that?"

"I...well...I just, sort of, dreamt it, but I know this key goes to that door. Now, you're coming with me." Clara grabbed Sorin's hand.

Apparently, he wasn't scared in real life like in her dream, but he didn't seem to mind holding her hand. His hand was warm, and the touch of his skin sent sparks up her arm.

Clara stuck the key in the hole.

"It fits."

She turned the knob and opened the door.

Suddenly, a rough wind barreled from behind, shoving the two of them toward the door waiting at the end of the hallway. The door vanished before they hit it.

They fell downward, instead of sideways.

They screamed and plummeted; screamed and plummeted; and again. They stopped screaming when the doomed impact never came.

"What's going on?" Sorin asked.

"I don't know; it's like we're supposed to feel like we're falling, but we really aren't."

"I'd hate to see the end of this fall." As Sorin said that, they both stopped with the ground a foot below them. Suspended in the air for a few seconds, Clara wriggled about and then dropped.

"Well, that was pretty easy," Clara said. Endless hills of green grass and beautiful trees, all covered with glorious flowers, surrounded them.

Quaint stone cottages lined the cobblestone streets, and an immense ocean lay to the far right, dozens of pirate-like ships riding its gentle waves. In the distance, a castle towered up to touch the blue-gray sky, its tallest spears hiding in the misty cloud cover.

Paradise.

Sorin stood up beside Clara.

"What is this place?"

"It's where I belong."

"Good day to you, ma'am, sir. Please follow me; Author Brigglesburg would like to see you."

The high-pitched accented voice came from behind her. Turning, Clara found a small gentleman dressed in old English attire, bent in a bow. When he straightened, he only came to her shoulders.

"Who is Author Brigglesburg?" Clara asked.

"The ruler of the Land of Book, fair lady. I assumed you already knew, since you seem happy enough. This is where people like you and me and apparently your friend there and others who are something more than human reside, if we choose to." His gray, wavy hair fell to his shoulders, and he had violet eyes that complemented his happy grin. His ears reached for the sky in a fight to see which one could be the more pointed.

Up a hill, they climbed to the grand castle crowning its summit, reminiscent of the European fortresses Clara had seen in her history books. As they ascended the stairs, trumpets blared, a most welcoming melody. Everything fit perfectly. She smiled and gripped Sorin's hand; he squeezed back.

"Welcome, Clara and Sorin. We appreciate that you have graced us with your presence. Please have a seat." Suddenly, two extravagant chairs appeared in front of the gigantic jewel-encrusted throne where a handsome older King sat. A warrior in his younger days, apparent from the battle scars marring his skin, but his earthly and wild presence was still calming as his eyes held theirs in a gentle recognition.

"Hi…um…where are we?" Clara asked, the only coherent thought she could force out of her mouth.

"Why my dears, you are in The Land of Book. I thought most definitely that Nigel here would have told you that by now."

"I touched on it, Sir."

"Very well. Then you already know. But do you understand why you're here?"

Awestruck, Clara stared at a huge lion, twice as big as any she had seen at a zoo, who padded into the room and sprawled by the King's throne, licking its paws lazily.

"No, sir, we don't," Sorin answered for her.

"You are here because you do not blend with the humans inhabiting Earth. As the true incarnations of book characters, you were meant to be written on paper, not alive and breathing, but ever since Lord Mondego tore the fabric of reality, spilling our lives into Earth's dimension, a child is born when a writer creates a new character.

"Every character has a choice. They can stay in the human world, or they can come here and live, but you only get one chance. You have found a portal in, which means it's time for you to choose. But I am a kind King, and I want my kingdom to love me. I always give characters time to decide. Visit as many times as you would like, but in three days, you must choose."

Clara couldn't speak, feeling hot all over. Her mind raced through her memories of everyone she loved, everyone that loved her, and the pain of being an outcast.

"Uh, okay, but how do we know who we are, I mean, what character are we?" Sorin asked as he blinked excessively and gulped several times in succession.

"Well, we know who you are, but you will not know until you have chosen, and usually, the character has to stay here to find out. Unless they research on Earth," the King answered.

"Okay." Clara considered finding out who she was before making her decision.

"The Land of Book offers many benefits. Immortality, the chance to live your own story, the opportunity to experience other stories—all at your fingertips. Choose wisely, my dears."

Clara thought she would miss her family desperately if she chose to go back to paradise. Unloading a few bags of groceries in the kitchen, Clara and her mom eased around each other in a silly small-kitchen-dance.

"You're such a sweetie, helping out the way you do. You don't know how much I appreciate you."

Her mother's smile wrenched her heart. Feeling like she had betrayed her family, Clara stamped out all thoughts of the Land of Book from her mind.

"What's wrong, dear?"

"Nothing, Mom. What's in that bag?" Clara pointed at a large brown paper bag that her mother guarded.

"Treats. I got the job!"

Clara momentarily jumped up and down with her mom in a circle of celebration.

"That's great. We should celebrate."

The celebration was a grand one indeed. If her mom hadn't gotten the job, the landlord would have evicted them soon. Clara got out the good plates, old and chipped, but they still had colorful butterfly patterns on them, and her sister lit candles. Nana put on the music and hobbled around setting the table. Then they all sat down to a dinner of sloppy joes and French fries, a sumptuous feast when they had faced starvation.

That night, Clara's mother tucked the covers around her shoulders and brushed the hair from her face. "Go; you'll be happy there."

"Mom, you know, don't you?"

"Yes, dear, I had to make that choice myself, as well as your grandmother and so many before her. We were different though, the choice came too late for us, but you have the chance now, before falling in love and molding a family. You decide whatever is right for you. No second chances."

"But how do I know?"

"Honey, you knew the moment you were there; just act on it. Don't worry about us; we will be fine. And maybe one day, you will see your sister there too."

"Okay, goodnight, Mom."

When Clara woke up, she knew what she had to do.

She got ready for school and packed a few extra things in her backpack, some mementos, her favorite books. She kissed and hugged her family. Twice. And then left the house. The air felt lighter. She was ready.

Sorin waited for her on the sidewalk. Seeing him, she felt as though she breathed for the first time. She glanced at him shyly, smiling, and then looked down at her shoes.

"Hi, Clara-Bell. You ready?"

"Yep, are you?"

"Definitely." His voice calmed her nerves. Glancing up to see his grin, she grinned back.

By Clara's second class, it appeared that her old friends had lost their snickering humor; they no longer looked at her with those sly smiles.

Later, Kate pulled a note from her pocket, read it, and then ran crying from the room. Whatever the problem, Clara thanked the stars she wasn't involved in their mess anymore.

At lunch, Sorin and Clara snuck to the old auditorium again.

"Did you see the argument?" Sorin asked.

"No."

"Lucas Sheldon told someone Lara had confessed her love for him, and that person spread a few rumors about it, so Lara confronted him but had to leave because she was crying so much."

"What? Are you serious?"

"They all turned on each other, and Kate told people about Eliza's baby persona; kids cooed and stuff at her. Classic! Then, Eliza told everyone Kate slept around, so she fled in tears. Camber...well, her boyfriend dumped her and told everyone it was because she couldn't hold a decent conversation. Not that it's funny, but it's some sort of payback."

"At least, I didn't do anything; it would've only made me as bad as them."

To Clara, it was a perfect case of karma.

"Are you ready?"

Sorin nodded, then yanked Clara against him and kissed her as he held her. She could feel her blood heating at his touch, his lips tasted like fresh mint. He smelled of soap and joy. She raked her fingers through his soft tousled black hair.

"I've wanted to do that for a while now."

"I'm glad you finally did."

"I have to confess I've crushed on you since the sixth grade." Sorin traced the edges of her face with soft fingers.

"Good for you; I *just* figured out that I have a crush on you."

"Good for you that I'm forgiving." He winked and took the key from her hand. Together, they turned the knob and stepped into the place they belonged.

# SURVIVAL
## Jaimey Grant

*A life for a life is the key to survival.*

**W**hen one life begins, another must end. It is the key to the planet's survival.

The key.

The only way.

Survival.

She was the key to the planet's survival.

Faolyne chanted the words as she ran, chanted them on her way to her next mark. The tails of her black cloak flapped behind her like the wings of a raven. Trees flew by, each a blur in the silent forest. She focused on nothing but her goal.

A human life waited at the end of the path, the one whose death would balance the shift and appease the gods. Specifically, appease Faolyne's dark master.

She did her master's bidding in the knowledge that should she fail, the world would be destroyed. The reason for such a contract remained a mystery, and Faolyne never questioned her fate or that of the world.

Slowing, she edged her way into the village. Small hovels, the homes of the townsfolk, surrounded a dusty square. Narrow alleys separated the small buildings. She slipped between them and sauntered into the square.

Deathly silence permeated the air. The irony was not lost on Faolyne, and a dark chuckle slipped past her red lips. The sound shivered over the land. She heard murmurings behind closed doors, the telltale creak of movement heralding the swift arrival of the curious.

Villagers emerged, their downtrodden faces wreathed with curiosity, a few with dread. They understood who and what the strange black-clad woman was, and some welcomed her in their hearts, hoping she would relieve them of their suffering.

"Mistress Denai!"

Faolyne's shout reverberated through the village, bouncing off walls and shooting up into the sky. A chill wind caught her white hair, swirling around sharp features and masking her cold black eyes. Legs apart and back straight, she waited, alert and ready.

At the name chosen, a collective gasp rose from the crowd. A few villagers wandered off, too old or sick to care for anything other than the fact that their luck remained unchanged.

A girl appeared in the doorway of a small abode, the neatness of which was a testament to her pride in, and love for, her home. That pride continued in her personal appearance; two perfect blond braids coiled on her head and a perfect, clean gown of the palest blue covered her perfect form. Her mother stood just behind, a protective presence in the shadows beyond the doorway.

Faolyne stared. Such a perfect specimen rarely became the master's desire. He cleansed the planet by sending her for the elderly, sick or injured. He expected her to slay this *child*? Surely, he had made a mistake in selecting the young and beautiful Denai...

Then Faolyne understood, hot rage suffusing her muscular form. She tensed, ready to spring. If the master wanted her to prove her worth, so be it. She would obey.

The mother stepped forward and pushed her daughter back, the protective gesture hiding everything but the girl's face. "I am the one you seek."

"You are not Denai. You seek to protect her."

"You speak the truth. I am Denai." A young voice, on the edge of womanhood, trembled across the square. The young woman stepped out of her mother's protection, her light eyes sweeping over Faolyne. Her face held a certain unnerving confidence. One would never know death courted her.

"It is your time," Faolyne told her. Her voice held an eerie tone rumbling from within, like an echo from the deepest pit of the Underworld. A shudder, like a dank chill emanating from warm bodies, spread through the gathered townspeople. Indrawn breaths and mutters surrounded them.

Faolyne's lips parted in a sneer, sharp white teeth peeking through. Her audience's reaction satisfied her. As long as they feared her, they would not challenge her. She could only hope the girl's intelligence prevented something as stupid as a defense.

Denai stiffened, fingers clenching in her skirts. "My time?"

"I am the Reaper Faolyne. A child draws breath in the lower country. You must die to balance the shift and guarantee the planet's survival."

"You are the key to survival, Reaper Faolyne?" At Faolyne's nod of assent, Denai added, "Then the planet will die because I will not."

Her hand shot up and silver streaked the air. Faolyne's body jerked, shock spreading through her. She looked down at the points of a razor-sharp star protruding from her torso. Warmth welled up around it, unseen in the darkness of her clothing and cloak. The villagers' eyes stared wide, their mouths hanging open.

Reaching up, Faolyne felt the weapon embedded in her chest and took a halting step forward. Her breath came in pain-filled gasps. Defeated by a girl and her own overconfidence.

Faolyne laughed, finally understanding the real reason behind her master's choice. Denai didn't exist to test the Reaper. She held a far greater purpose.

Denai swept across the square and confronted the dying Reaper, her pale form wavering in

Faolyne's vision like a phantom. In one hand, she held another shiny silver star.

"You are defeated."

"It is so. You have acted in the manner the master expected," Faolyne whispered.

Denai frowned, her lip curling in contempt. "One should expect a battle when death comes to call. Your tyranny is at an end. You can no longer make us suffer your whims."

"*You* will suffer. The reaper is key to the world's survival." The copper tang of blood swirled in her mouth and spilled past her lips. Faolyne coughed, impatiently wiping it away. Her black-clad arm glistened with moisture.

"Death is no more. You can no longer hurt us." Denai straightened, uncertainty coating her words. The townsfolk backed away, muttering.

"There must always be a Reaper," Faolyne insisted. She fell to her knees and pulled the star from her chest. Her body shuddered and stiffened, falling back to lie on the dusty ground, her mouth open in a silent scream.

**D**enai stood over the woman, hands on her hips, smiling. She had won, saving her people.

Faolyne released another gargled laugh. The sound strangled in blood before it reached completion. Her leg shot out, knocking Denai off balance. She sprawled on the ground in an inelegant heap.

Denai clutched at the graceful fingers wrapping around her throat, pulling her close to the Reaper's face. Faolyne choked, turning her head to spit a scarlet stream. Denai inwardly recoiled, horrified. Had she really done this?

Faolyne turned back to Denai, the smell of death and decay swirled in each word that exited her bloodstained lips.

"Take heed, killer of death. Your time for suffering is nigh. Your new master waits."

"You are finished. Death is no more," Denai insisted, her voice forced beyond the restraining fingers at her throat. Her mind struggled for the reason behind the Reaper's taunts, striving to understand why her body chilled while her panic grew.

"Foolish girl! I was not the first."

Denai barely heard the ragged whisper before everything went black. Grabbing her head, she screamed. Immense pressure exploded inside her mind, roared in her ears, and burned her lungs with every breath. Then the shadows receded.

Whimpering, she opened her eyes. The sun still glinted through the trees high overhead, and Faolyne's body lay beside her, empty eyes accusing her. The harsh face smiled softly, as if she had found peace. A pang of guilt rolled over Denai; the reaper had been human. In destroying the one who wreaked havoc on the planet, she had destroyed death. Why did she feel sorry for the creature who needed to die?

Denai pushed herself up, the hand at her neck falling away. The crowd whispered and pointed at her, but fell back a step whenever she met their eyes. Her mother knelt just out of reach, her crumpled face streaked with tears. "No, no. Not you, Denai. My child, my child."

"Mother?" Denai reached for her, but the villagers grabbed her arms and pulled her away.

"Leave it be," they said.

The sky darkened as storm clouds rolled in. Rain pelted those assembled in the village square; they darted away, dragging her mother with them and leaving Denai alone. The moisture soaked her to the bone, and she sucked in a ragged breath.

The world shivered and cracked. A fissure opened, spewing forth a black cloud. Materializing within, a huge form emerged, shapeless in the dark mist yet having the form of a beautiful human male. As Denai's eyes fastened on the being, her mind flooded with pain. The pain moved and centered in her heart, ripping her apart. She clutched her chest.

"Come, Reaper."

The voice echoed, slithering around the human audience. The being stepped forward, his perfect beauty at odds with his evil calling. Denai waited for Faolyne to rise, waited for the Reaper to leave with her master. But nothing happened, and the dark lord's eyes remained fastened on Denai.

Her heart stuttered in her chest, the air leaving her lungs in a panicked whoosh. Through a haze, she saw her mother break free of the villagers and try desperately to reach her, but an unseen force in the mist blocked her. In that moment, she knew.

He wasn't there for Faolyne.

He was there for her.

Her feet stumbled forward toward her destiny.

When one life begins, another must end. It is the key to the planet's survival.

The key.

The only way.

Survival.

She was the key to the planet's survival.

Denai chanted the words as she ran, chanted them on her way to her next mark.

# UNLOCKING WILLIAM

## Jeanne Voelker

*The whole school is weary of William's antics,*
*but will he ever tire of them?*

My name is Graham, but my best friend William, er, I mean Billiam, insists on calling me Grasshopper. In fact, everyone calls me Grasshopper.

Band, the first period of the day, forces my sleepy brain cells to wake up whether they want to or not. I don't mind though, because I work hard to be first clarinet, and someday—if I'm lucky—I'll be president of the high school band. Not that I'm stuck-up or anything; I just love music.

Friday morning, the fourth time through *Bugler's Holiday*, Billiam, on third-part trumpet, still played B-natural on all of the B-flat notes. No one laughed out loud, but a few snickered. Mr. Hector the Director signaled cut.

"William, let's hear it from the beginning of section three, slowww-ly."

"Just me?"

"Just you."

Billiam played the passage, and this time he overblew the high note. The class laughed and Mr. Hector tapped his baton on the music stand to signal quiet.

"William, how many times this week have you practiced?"

"Uh, well, I haven't taken my trumpet home this week. I had too much to carry."

"*Bugler's Holiday* is a show piece for trumpet trio. The expectation in this class is that everyone will practice."

"Okay."

"Okay you'll practice?"

"Er, yeah."

"Good... Now, class, let's play the *Colonel Bogey March*."

Band practice continued normally until Billiam threw a crumpled piece of notebook paper into the horn of the Sousaphone; that's when Mr. Hector lost his cool. "I'm going to call your parents, William. And I think I'm not the only teacher who will be telephoning today."

"She won't be home," said Billiam.

"We have the office number," said Mr. Hector.

Sometimes, I wanted to be as nonchalant as Billiam. Other times, I wanted to smack him.

After band, Billiam and I went to our shared locker and crammed his trumpet case and my clarinet case in with our mess of papers. As we overtook Traci and Jill in the hallway, Billiam snapped Traci's bra strap, then cruised on by, leaving me to take the blame.

"Knock it off, Grasshopper!"

I stared back at her. Traci should know by now who did it. As we passed another clutch of girls, Billiam licked his thumb and pressed it to Nanci's ear.

Nanci said, "Stop it!"

Her friends made gagging sounds.

"Ewww, wet willy!"

"Gross!"

This time it was obvious who did it, so I got to laugh. Billiam still wore a smirk as we passed the Josef Boyde Middle School display case, home of the stuffed jay boid.

In history class, while Mr. Schroeder lectured, Billiam passed notes to Kim. He tapped Mary on the shoulder, but she ignored him.

I just smiled and shook my head.

At lunch, Billiam jumped in ahead of the other kids in line. No one challenged him since he's bigger than everyone else.

I almost choked on my milk when he performed mashed-potato catapult shots the length of the lunch table to Bobert's mouth. Jill and Effie watched so Billiam invented some fancy lob shots and a missile shot.

"Look at this missile-shot, Effer!"

This was pretty funny until Billiam mash-potatoed Bobert's eye. The lunch teacher came over to scold us, but no one listens to Mrs. Lump. Her real name is Mrs. Lumstrom, but her style of teaching is to sit at her desk while the students work. Mrs. Lump doesn't know we call her Lump—just as our principal, Truman North, doesn't know we call him True North.

Fourth period, I had gym class, which I like except for the sweaty tennis shoe smell. I saw the basketball hoop all bent down. It didn't look fixable, so someone was in trouble.

During fifth period, the last class of the day, Billiam accidentally livened up our pre-algebra class. The room was quiet until Billiam dropped a handful of ball bearings on the floor. He said he didn't mean to, and I believe him, but Mr. O'Brien, our math teacher, told him to shape up.

Another teacher came in, and I overheard them whispering that someone during lunch hour had bent the basketball hoop in the gym. I glanced at Billiam. Did he go to the gym after lunch? The corners of Billiam's mouth turned down, and his eyes watched the teachers as he shrank low in his seat.

After class, as we walked to our locker, I remembered what Mr. Hector had said about telephoning Billiam's mother.

"Do you think they'll call?"

"Naw, if they haven't called by three o'clock, they won't," he said, but his voice didn't sound so sure.

First period Monday morning, I noodled on my clarinet while other kids warmed up in their own way. Mr. Hector tapped his plastic baton on his music stand.

"Okay, let's tune to first clarinet…"

I gave them an "A". As Mr. Hector tuned our section, the band-room door opened and in came a woman who stood taller than any teacher and upright as a post. She wore a black business suit and high-heel shoes. Gold earrings bobbed beneath her lacquered hair and a multitude of keys jangled from her key ring as she stuffed it into her purse. She must have keys to half the town.

The tuning faded as the woman strode to Mr. Hector, the heels of her shoes clicking on the uncarpeted floor.

"I'm William's mother...we spoke on the phone, but it's nice to meet you in person. I'll be sitting in the back of the room today."

All the kids looked at Billiam. Billiam looked at the floor.

When we played *Bugler's Holiday*, Billiam hit the right notes, but not smoothly. Mr. Hector said, "That was better, William, but it still needs more home practice. The tone should be crisp and bright."

After band, we took our instruments to our locker and went straight to history class. As soon as the class settled, Billiam's mother appeared, introduced herself to Mr. Schroeder, and took a seat at the back of the class. Billiam didn't pass any notes. He just sat there with his eyes down. his mother said the same thing in every class.

Billiam was unusually quiet, as were we all. At snack time, his mother stood near the junk food machines with her arms folded. At the noon break, she sat next to Billiam and ate school lunch with him. The rest of us sat at tables nearby, and knew that we, too, were being watched.

During last period, Billiam started to relax and tease the kid next to him. His mother rose from her chair, clamped her big hand on his shoulder, and gave him a *look*. He sank into his chair.

That's how it went Monday through Thursday. She watched him like a mother hawk. Once when she saw Dickard try to trip a kid carrying a lunch tray, Billiam's mother said, "Richard, I know your parents, and I have their phone number."

Monday to Thursday, I couldn't relax until the day was over and Billiam's mother took him home.

For two weeks, the eighth-graders had practiced jokes, songs, and soft-shoe dances for Friday's vaudeville show. We would perform for the sixth and seventh grade students. Billiam and I had rehearsed the 'Camptown Races' song and had also prepared our surprise version—without the knowledge of our pianist. He would be surprised too. I worried we might have to change our plan, but I didn't see Billiam's mother at band practice on Friday.

"Where's your mom?"

"She went back to work. She said our summer vacation is now four days shorter, and she doesn't want to miss five days. Anyway, now we can do our surprise duet."

"Do you think we should?"

"Of course we should. It's funnier than the original."

"What if we get in trouble?"

"Trouble? No, the teachers don't listen. Anyway, vaudeville was like that—song parodies that make fun of people."

Bucky is our pianist. For a little kid with funny teeth and big feet, he sure is good on the piano. He can play Mozart pieces with his eyes closed, and he's a good accompanist too.

As students shuffled into the auditorium, teachers stationed themselves at vantage points. Billiam and I would be last on the program, after the jokes and skits and other songs. After we sang "Camptown Races", Bucky would transition us into Al Jolson's "Sewanee", which we have changed into a school song with dance steps.

Before the program could start, Mr. Truman North, our principal, gave his usual welcome speech, but there was one difference.

"We have a guest in our audience today. Mr. Young, the Superintendent of Schools, came by earlier, and I invited him to join us for some traditional vaudeville. The eighth grade students will perform for us. They have studied this historical form of theatre that trained many of the great actors and comedians of the twentieth century."

He paused for a response, so we applauded.

"Let's show our superintendent a fine performance and an appreciative audience."

My stomach felt like a roller-coaster ride and I looked at Billiam, but if he was feeling any stress, he didn't show it. His eyes shone, and he seemed ready to go on stage.

The curtain rose to a pantomime-dance with recorded music. Kim, Grace Chin, and Mary George performed a galloping pony-express dance. Billiam leaned toward me and said, "There's a time problem here. It looks like they're riding horses to show an American history theme, but the music is from The Grand Canyon Suite which is twentieth century."

"It's not their fault. The teachers chose the songs," I answered.

"They could have asked Mr. Hector. He would have chosen better."

"You would blow them away if you ever let on how much you know. You don't have to hide it you know."

"And waste my genius on a lousy classroom? Never."

One of the teacher-monitors shushed us, ending our commentary.

The performance moved on to school jokes with Bobert and Tina.

Tina began. "If I give you two rabbits and two rabbits and another two rabbits, how many rabbits have you got?"

"Seven!" Bobert answered.

"No, listen carefully again. If I give you two rabbits and two rabbits and another two rabbits, how many rabbits have you got?"

"Seven!"

"Let's try this another way. If I give you two apples and two apples and another two apples, how many apples have you got?"

"Six."

"Good. Now if I give you two rabbits and two rabbits and another two rabbits, how many rabbits have you got?"

"Seven!"

"How on earth do you work out that three lots of two rabbits are seven?" asked Tina.

"I've already got one rabbit at home!"

The audience laughed and a few people clapped.

"Isn't the principal a dummy!" said Bobert.

"Well, do you know who I am?" asked Tina.

"No."

"I'm the principal's daughter."

"And do you know who I am?" asked Bobert.

"No."

"Thank goodness!"

This got a bigger laugh from the audience, and someone whistled.

Four more acts—everyone in eighth grade played in one of the songs, skits, or joke segments.

Finally, the time came for Billiam and me to sing. The kids in the audience squirmed, and their chairs squeaked. Bucky strode up to the piano. Billiam swaggered right behind—and I followed, wondering if we oughta play it safe and sing the traditional words. But no, Billiam said vaudeville was known for parody and ethnic jokes—the works. He gave me a look that said I had better not chicken out. He knew he could count on Bucky, even though Bucky didn't know what we planned to do. Bucky would follow Billiam's lead.

Bucky played the intro to Camptown Races and we sang:

*Camptown Races sing dis song.*
*Doo dah doo dah*
*Teacher's in de bafroom all day long*
*Oh doo dah day*

A collective chuckle spread through the audience, and the chair squeaking stopped...

*Why he on de bafroom floor?*
*Doo dah doo dah*
*Drank too much de night before*
*Oh doo dah day*

*Ax the principal to make him stop*
*Doo dah doo dah*
*Bring de janitor and de mop*
*Oh de doo dah day*

Now the students were all ears and snickers, so we plowed on to the chorus...

*Gwine to party all night*
*Gwine to be sick all day*
*Bet my money on de teacher's wife*
*She gonna make him pay*

By this time the kids were laughing, and I didn't dare look at the teachers. We went right on to the ethnic verses…

*Yonny Yonson had a farm*
*Doo dah doo dah*
*Laszlo Zuto made whiskey in de barn*
*All de live-long day (all day)*

*Yonny went to de barn one day*
 *Doo dah doo dah*
*Effer and Bucko wuz rollin' in de hay*
*All de doo dah day (all day)*

In the front row, Effie ducked her head as the kids around her pointed and laughed. But at this point, Bucky played a wrong chord and nearly stumbled our tempo. So I concentrated on the song while he picked it up, and off we went…

*Gwine ter roll all night*
*Gwine ter roll all day*

Next part is spoken so we belted it in order to be heard over the accompaniment...

*First came Love*
*Then came Marriage,*
*Now they're pushin' a baby carriage!*

The audience howled and stamped their feet. I saw Mr. Schroeder hushing students in the back of the auditorium and Mr. O'Brien making his way toward the stage.

Luckily, we had completed the pre-arranged number of doo-dah verses, so Bucky transitioned us to our next song—a song the teachers could not object to. With chord changes and a short intro, off we went with our own school-spirit version of Al Jolson's "Sewanee, how I love ya, how I love ya."

*Josef Boyde Middle School,*
*How I love ya, How I love ya,*

*My dear old Jay Boyde*
*I'd give the world <clap> to <clap> be*
*<shuffle, clap>*
*Right back in J-O-S-E-F B-O-Y-D-E*
*And oh my Mammy's waitin' for me,*
*Prayin' for me down by old Jay Boyde*
*That I will tread these boards no more*
*When I grad-u-ate from Jay Boyde school*

As planned, Bucky played a short reprise, and Billiam and I did our soft-shoe dance in which we incorporated some jay bird imitations. But no one paid attention to us, for all the students were on their feet, clapping and dancing.

On Monday, the school buzzed with the news that the school mascot was missing from the locked display case in the front hall. Where was our preserved feathered friend? The truant bird mystery stimulated the imaginations of students and staff.

That afternoon, Billiam and I were called into the principal's office. Mr. North stared over his glasses at us.

"Your vaudeville song changes were generally well-received by the students, but you didn't clear them with the faculty."

"We were trying to make them funnier for the students," said Billiam.

"How did the named students feel about the stereotype jokes and inappropriate dialect?"

Billiam said, "I researched the history of vaudeville and ethnic jokes were traditional."

"Yes," said Mr. North. "Traditionally, there were jokes aimed at ethnic groups. They made humorous observations about cultural differences, and these served to make ethnic groups cohesive, but they weren't insulting and individual people were not singled out."

"We didn't mean to hurt anyone's feelings," I said.

Mr. North cleared his throat and then smiled at us. "If you simply hope they didn't mind, you might never know whether or not they were offended. I think you need to be more proactive here. What could you do to ease the feelings of the students you named?"

"We could say we didn't mean it," Billiam said.

"Sometimes it's not what a person says, but how they say it."

"I don't understand," said Billiam.

"Okay, what if you said, 'I hope you weren't offended because we didn't mean to hurt anyone's feelings.' How might the person feel about that?"

"They might think it's okay. Or, they might think I was saying they shouldn't have been offended...so if they were offended, they were in the wrong?"

"Right, and how would they feel if you just apologized?"

"I guess they would feel that *we* were in the wrong," said Billiam.

"*Were* you in the wrong?"

"We just meant to be funny."

"William, it's not my job to force you to apologize. You're old enough to make your own decisions. But it's the right thing to do, and I think it would clear the air and help everyone's friendships. A simple apology—'I'm sorry we named you and some other students in our silly song, and if I embarrassed you or made you feel bad, I'm very sorry.' It needn't be a public announcement. A private apology will do. What do you think?"

"I think it's probably a good idea," said Billiam, and I said I would apologize too.

I thought Mr. North was finished with us so I stood up to leave.

"Wait, there's news I want to share with both of you," said Mr. North. I sat back down.

"There are five months of school until summer break—in September, you'll go to high school. I think you are boys who like a challenge and will often take the initiative to set a challenge for yourselves."

What could we answer? 'Yes' might sound like a confession. 'No' would sound like a denial. But Mr. North didn't ask for an answer. He continued with his observations.

"I see you are 'B' students—not bad, but I think you can do better. I think you boys have leadership potential. Some young people need a larger arena than middle school, and it's right that students outgrow their junior-high environment. Your world *should* grow larger."

Mr. North pulled a shiny gold key from his pocket and unlocked his desk drawer. He pulled out some papers with colored photos—some sort of travel brochures.

"I want to give you advance notice about a program that is offered early in high school. A tour of Europe, for selected students, will be scheduled at the end of your freshman year. The application is due in September, so acceptance to the program is based on your eighth grade performance. Student ambassadors will be chosen on the basis of grades, teacher recommendations, curiosity, and responsibility. Students with a more mature outlook, who are ready to learn something from other cultures, have a good chance at this, but the trip is limited to twenty students of the two hundred who will be in your freshman class. Students who travel will be representing their schools and their country. Does this sound like something that would interest you?"

Billiam said, "It sounds awesome, but my mother can't afford to send me on an international trip."

"You would need your mother's permission to go, but she wouldn't have to pay for the trip. The high school organizes all-school fundraisers to cover most of the expense. Students who help with the fundraising earn credit toward their application if they apply to travel the following year. We will soon announce this to all of the school, but I wanted to tell you boys now. I would like you to think about the opportunities ahead. The trip I mentioned is just one of them—there are many for students who give their best."

Mr. North stood up from his desk to walk us to the door.

"I understand there's going to be a band concert next weekend, and I've heard that *Bugler's Holiday* is on the program. Are you ready for it?"

"Oh yes, sir, we're ready! I hope you'll come hear us!" said Billiam.

Mr. True North smiled. "I'll be there."

On the way back to class, Billiam said, "I want to try for the trip. How about you?

"Sure, it sounds terrific! Do you want to hang out after school today?"

"Naw, I gotta do homework."

The stuffed jay bird reappeared, perched on the branch in the Josef Boyde Middle School display case. The case was always locked, so no one knew how the jay left or how it returned. Traci said the jay came to life at night and foraged for food. Some kids thought a teacher had taken it, and some thought a student had. But if it was stolen, why was it returned?

And why would anyone steal a ratty jay bird anyway? Jay boid's feathers looked brighter after his return, and his crest had been straightened. I thought maybe the janitor had removed the bird to clean its feathers, but I asked him and he said he hadn't.

As I pondered the mystery of the jay bird, I suspected Billiam might know something, but he hadn't said a word. Finally, on the day of our concert, I had a chance to ask.

"What do you think happened? Do you think the janitor took the bird to clean it?"

"He said he didn't."

"Then...how did the bird disappear and return?"

"Oh, I dunno. Maybe someone found a way to steal it, then changed his mind. People do change their minds sometimes."

I thought about this for a moment. "If they always keep the case locked, then putting the jay back must have been as hard as taking it."

Billiam glanced sideways before he replied, "Yes, even harder."

# SHOSHANNA
## K. G. Borland

*Some rules should never be broken.*

The last of the Alori arrived at the gatehouse, and I turned to face Gabriel, who blocked the pass to the human world.

"What are the three Cardinal Laws we follow when we leave the Home?" Gabriel shouted over the excited crowd, too busy shoving, laughing, and joking to pay any attention.

"I will not repeat myself, now answer my question or there will be no trip today."

"Calm down, Gabriel. Why are you always such a stickler for protocol?" I pushed through the crowd, accidentally hitting someone in the face with my ebony wings. "Oh! My bad, man."

Gabriel clenched his fists. "You can never be too careful, Jayson; making sure you all remember puts me at ease, so can we *please* recite the laws before we cross the boundary?"

"Fine. The sooner we do this, the faster I get away from you." With a mock bow, I turned to the flock's youth and raised my arms like a conductor. "All together now, everyone, and make it believable for the stickler's sake." A chuckle rippled through the group as I swung my arms, and we recited the three sacred laws:

*The Alori shall never reveal their wings.*

*The Alori shall never speak the sacred tongue outside the Home.*

*The Alori shall never converse with a human except to secure provisions for the flock.*

I turned to Gabriel. "Satisfied?"

"It'll do." Everyone cheered, and Gabriel tried to quiet them one last time. "Alright, let's cross the barrier everyone. In an orderly fashion please."

The youth nearly ran him over getting out of the Home's invisible boundary, their clothes instantly changing into human-acceptable apparel, t-shirts and blue jeans.

But not me. No, I'd thought about this day for far too long to arrive in the same old clothes. A ripple started at my feet the moment I crossed the threshold, my clothes changing to a white t-shirt, dark-print blue jeans, and a leather jacket. "Yeah, that's more like it."

"Hold up, Jayson. That is not appropriate attire."

"It is my seventeenth season; I can do whatever I want. C'mon, let me go."

Gabriel ran his hand through his hair. "Look, I know you're excited about your seventeenth season, but *please* be careful. I don't want you getting hurt on your first time out alone—"

"—or worse, putting the flock in jeopardy." I finished the lecture we'd heard a million times.

Gabriel shooed the rest of the group away, but when he turned back, his eyes were wet with tears. "You think I care more about the flock than you getting hurt? You're the first Alori to *ever* go on this excursion alone."

Powdery dander fell from his wings like glitter as I patted him on the back. "Chill, Gabe. I know you wouldn't want anything to happen to me, I'm just giving you a hard time—you know, like we always *used* to before you became a stuffed shirt."

Gabriel pushed me off. "Being chosen to be part of the guard is an honor, and you should watch your tongue. You're probably next on the recruitment list. Just be careful."

"Aren't I always?" I said.

"Jay, I'm serious. You're my best friend. I don't know what I'd do if…" Gabe looked down at his feet.

"Gabe, relax." Jogging back a few steps, I faced the human world. "See ya, man. Keep the kids safe, alright? I need nestlings to pick on when I get back."

I walked into the Eastchase Shopping Centre full of energy. What seemed like thousands of humans bustled through the restaurants, stores, and parking lots.

At a small food distributor called *Panera Bread*, I ordered a Caesar Wrap from the human behind the counter, who sweated profusely despite the heavy artificial air their species pumped into the building. I swerved to leave but knocked into a girl. We both spilled our meals over each other. Unfortunately for me, hers was a hot bread bowl of chicken soup.

"Oh gosh! I am so sorry! I think I burned you. I'm such spazz!" The girl dabbed her napkin in her soft drink and placed the wet paper on my hands.

"Don't worry about it. I'll get some ice from the counter." I smiled at her hoping that would be the end of it; those simple sentences had already broken one of the Cardinal Laws: *Never converse with a human except to secure provisions for the flock.*

"Nonsense! You go back to your table, and I'll pay for a new wrap and soup. It's the least I can do." She looked down at my hand, bright red for the burns. "And I'll get you that ice."

She seemed so hopeful; I couldn't refuse. Besides, humans were noted for their stubborn nature, and this one looked especially determined. "Alright, I'll see you at my table." About five minutes later, she arrived with our new food and a towel with ice in it.

"Do you mind if I eat with you? I know I just dumped blazing hot soup on you, but the lunch rush came and I lost my table. The rest are taken."

I made the mistake of looking up into her eyes—had I ever seen such beauty? Three colors ringed her iris: a deep green bordered the outside, encircling a bright green, which encompassed a green so pale, it almost seemed white against the black depths of her pupil. Scarlet hair fell in waves over her shoulders, and a single curl bobbed against her cheek.

"No."

"Oh sorry..." Her eyes sank and she turned to leave.

I grabbed her hand and smiled. "Wait. I mean 'no, I don't mind', not 'no, you can't sit here'. Please. Sit."

She slid into the seat, fixed her napkin on her lap, and grinned like a cat. "So what's your name?"

"Jayson, what's yours?"

"Shoshanna."

"It's a very pretty name."

"I never really liked it. It's Hebrew or something like that. I just have everyone call me Sho." She took a sip out of her soda.

"Sho it is then." I took a bite out of my wrap pondering more conversation and grasped for more topics. "So what do you do for a living?"

"I'm a student in high school, aren't you?" She laughed and I tried to laugh with her, but it came out more like a cough. Eyeing me critically, she said, "You're not one of those drop-outs, are you?"

"Uh, no. Um, I go to school in a neighboring county." I focused on keeping my face blank as I waited for her reaction to my almost-truth. Nearby county indeed, just a hop, skip, and a jump across the border to a whole different world.

"Me too! I'm just here to go shopping. My town doesn't have half the stores there are here. Sure they've added a few, but not enough." She was so intense—her brows furrowed and her nose squinted but in a cute way.

She jabbed her spoon in my direction. "What's that look for?"

"What look?"

"You're looking at me with a smirk."

"I like the way you squint when you talk. It's very becoming."

Her cheeks turned a bright red, and she moved her head into her shoulder. "Geez. Don't hold back or anything. Just say what you think why don't ya."

"Are you blushing?"

"Well what do you expect? A cute guy tells me I'm pretty—yeah, I'm going to be flattered." She giggled.

I could feel my own face heating as she stared at me with those intriguing eyes. "Sorry if I embarrassed you. Sometimes I say what comes to mind before I think about it."

"Flattery will get you everywhere, but if you're not careful, you'll get my hopes up."

"Hopes up for what?"

"That you'll say yes to having dinner with me tonight. Say around seven-ish?" Sho flipped her hair back and stood up.

"Where are you going?"

"Well its three o'clock now correct?"

Looking over at the clock. "Yes, but—"

"And you want to meet for dinner at seven?" She picked up her tray.

I nodded.

"Well, that's why I have to leave." She walked over to the trash can while I sat at our table confused. Had I just agreed to a date with a human? When she came back to push her chair under the table, she said, "I have to leave because I have to go get ready for this hot date at seven o'clock; we're going to Marchelle's downtown. It's fantastic!"

She radiated such life; it was impossible to resist. I caved and flirted back. "Are you now? So Marchelle's is in downtown, and you'll be there with some 'hot date' around seven?"

"Yup," she said.

"It's too bad I can't meet you."

Her face fell, and I barely contained my laughter. "I have a date in town with this smoking hot red-head around seven as well."

Her face turned the color of her scarlet hair, and a radiant smile broke from behind her lips.

"Maybe we'll run into each other then."

"I'll make sure of it." I winked at her as she walked out the door, her face flushing red all over again.

I tried to feel guilty for breaking an unwritten Cardinal rule, *Never flirt/date with a human,* but watching her crimson mane bobbing away in the crowd, elation hummed inside me.

I smoothed out the creases in my leather jacket as I waited for her. My foot kept tapping the ground nervously and pedestrians walking by gave me awkward looks. My head down, I listened to their footsteps.

What if she didn't show up? My mind asked the same question over and over. Wouldn't that be for the best? The chances of the council finding out about my overstep would dwindle to none if she stood me up. Almost on cue, the sound of footsteps stopped right in front of me.

"Sorry I'm late. I got caught up in traffic. I swear this town has too many people for how small it is." I looked up to meet Shoshanna's face. Her head tilted slightly to the side with a small smile. I couldn't help but smile back.

"Apology accepted. I just got here."

She snorted. "By the tapping of your foot when I was walking up, I'm going to guess you've been here since seven."

"You got me. I didn't want you to feel bad before our date even started."

She walked up to me and pulled on the edges of my jacket. "Well, your attempt is appreciated. I don't know about you, but I'm starving like nobody's business."

That got a laugh from me. "I could eat a horse myself."

She walked ahead of me putting an extra swing in her step. "That's good because Marchelle's got quite the selection tonight. Anything you could think of: beef, pork, lamb, chicken... and any other kind of bird you could think of."

I hesitated for a second because I thought I noticed a change in her demeanor, but she quickly turned around to show her smiling face.

I put my arm out for her to join as we entered the restaurant. "Lead on."

The moment that we walked into Marchelle's, Sho transformed into quite the social butterfly. "Mark! So nice to see you! It's been forever!" She unlinked arms with me and hugged the man. He looked like a lumberjack with his hefty beard and plaid shirt.

"Shoshanna! How is my favorite niece?"

"I'm good. So glad I'm finally on summer vacation; I thought junior year would never end!" She smiled up at her uncle.

"Come now, Shoshanna, introduce your dashing friend here." A woman I could've sworn wasn't there a second ago walked from behind Mark with her hand sliding on his shoulder. She was about half a foot shorter than him with wavy hair the same shade of red as Sho's.

Sho rolled her eyes. "How rude of me! Mom, this *dashing* young man is Jayson, and we are on a date. Jayson, this is my mom, Rachelle, and my uncle, Mark."

"Nice to meet you." I started to bow in the Alori way but caught myself and offered a hand.

As Rachelle's fingers closed around mine, my heart sped and my wings itched to be unfurled. My eyes darted about the room, searching for the danger setting off my fight or flight senses, but nothing seemed out of the ordinary.

A slow smile spread across her face, but before I could pinpoint exactly why I felt so threatened, Sho grabbed my arm and hauled me off to a table.

"Ignore her; she likes to intimidate all my dates."

"I heard that!" Rachelle called.

"You were meant to!" Sho hollered back. I couldn't help but laugh; she punched me playfully in the arm. "Hey! Don't laugh at the crazy family; we can't help ourselves."

She sat us at a private two-person table in the corner of the restaurant. The small violin band was far enough away the music was just the perfect volume to be a comforting back noise rather than an annoyance.

"I should have warned you the family might be here."

"It's fine, really."

Sho put her hand on my knee and leaned into me. The sides of our bodies lay against each other, and I was fully aware of every place our bodies touched. Tilting her neck to the side, she leaned closer to me. Reading the situation, I leaned into her, and our lips met. I traced my fingers up her arm, but she pulled away. Wiping her lips, she looked up to see her mother standing in an archway, watching us. Sho looked down in shame, or something else, I couldn't tell.

A young man with a white apron around his waist came over to our table. He looked at me with a grimace. "Here for *dinner?*"

"Tyler, stop. Bring us something special, please." Sho dismissed him with a nod, but his eyes lingered on me until my warning bells chimed in my senses again. A bead of sweat rolled down my forehead as he returned to the kitchen.

"Ex-boyfriend I'm guessing?"

"A couple times my ex actually. My parents want me to be with him, but I don't want him. It is just one of the many ways my parents force me to do things I really *don't* want to do. Small towns don't offer much variety. At least, not usually."

I couldn't read her expression, but I could swear I saw regret in the way she bit her lip. She shrugged, dispelling the odd thought. I fumbled with the napkin, and the silverware fell off the table. I reached down to catch them, but Shoshanna beat me to it. I blinked. "Wow. You've got some serious reflexes."

"I do what I can." She placed the silverware beside my plate, her body close enough I could feel her breath against my cheek.

I turned my face towards her, but she pulled away slowly dragging her hand across my chest as she did. No Alori had ever been so forward with me before. Everything about her teased my senses.

A different waiter came to our table, and in no time our food arrived.

"Ah, here we go, the house special. To a great night so far and more to come." She raised her glass for a toast.

I raised my glass with her, and we drank. The cool drink slid down my throat with a hint of lemon. I licked my lips. "What is this?"

"That's sweet tea, babe. Let's dig in." Tensing, she clutched her napkin and wrung it between her fists.

I choked on the tea; there on our plates lay two roasted Doves, sacred symbols of the Alori. To kill one was sacrilege enough, but she intended for us to *eat* them. My stomach churned as the bile rose in my throat.

"Something wrong?"

I flinched. "No, but I'm not feeling well. I think I need to go."

"Are you sure? This is really good." She lifted a wing to her lips and bit into the tender flesh, ripping the meat away from bone and sinew.

I fought to keep my revulsion from showing. The walls of the room pressed in on me, and my wings itched so badly I could feel them twitching beneath their covering. "Yeah, I'm sorry. I must've caught a bug or something. I need some air."

She studied me for a long moment and then snapped her fingers. "Fine, we'll go. Tyler! Box this up for me; I'll be back later for it."

She linked arms with me again and placed her other hand on my forearm as we walked past her family and then down to the riverbank tucked behind the restaurant. I felt like an idiot for my panic attack, but there were some things a guy couldn't explain on the first date, like I'm a different species and I have wings. Definitely second date information.

I gave her shoulders a squeeze. "I'm sorry; maybe next time I'll take you to one of my favorite restaurants."

"Oh, I don't think you'll have to worry about that."

"And why's that?"

She stopped us in a small clearing and moved to stand in front of me, both hands on my chest smiling up at me. She stood on her toes, wrapped her arms around my neck, and kissed me. The kiss was deep but quick, and she pulled away to lean into my ear. "You won't be alive for another date, my little *oiseau*."

"What?"

"My little *bird*."

My wings kicked against their confines, and I jerked back, but she had already moved away.

"Who are you, Shoshanna?"

"What no more 'Sho'?" She circled me, her lithe body predatory with deliberate steps, like something stalking its prey.

"I thought only your friends called you 'Sho'."

"You can't be friends with your meal? What kind of race are you Alori anyway? Didn't your mothers teach you to play with your food?" She lunged at me, her claws aimed at my face. Wait...*claws!*

My Alori training kicked in. I ducked down and threw her over my back. She reacted quickly and landed on her feet skidding to a stop on the leaves. She hissed, her body becoming more cat-like by the second. My wings strained against the leather jacket, but I dared not take my attention off her even if it meant flight.

"I guess a better question would be, *what* are you, Sho?"

"Aww, you're using 'Sho' again. So glad we could patch things up!" She lunged at me again, but this time I was ready. I dodged, grabbed her tail, and threw her against a tree.

She hit with a thud and slid to the ground. I felt a jolt of regret and took a step towards her when I heard loud growls and hisses from all around me. *"Get away from her!"*

I darted glances around me and then back at Sho who shook her head and got to her feet, a trickle of blood on the corner of her mouth. The first waiter from the restaurant, Tyler, crawled over to Sho and rubbed against her leg while sitting on all fours his tail swaying behind him.

She leaned down to his level and scratched his head, "I'm alright, Tyler. Shoshanna's alright. But we can't have Jayson yet; I have to share with the whole pard. They'll be here soon."

He purred. Both of them looked at me, their pupils in slits.

Tyler hunched, his bones cracking and his body arching. He screamed in pain, but that quickly became a roar. His fingers and feet balled up and then unfurled into claws. Arms and legs shortened and grew muscle. The horrific sounds immobilized me with their gruesomeness, bones cracking, skin tearing, and spilling from his pores, erupting fur made a plopping sound like wet feet on the tile floor. A minute later, where Tyler the human once stood, a fierce mountain lion rolled its shoulders, as if ready to pounce. Tyler roared, and a half-dozen nearby lions answered his summons.

Jerked out of my shock and inaction, I ripped my jacket off, but before I could take flight, the lions entered the clearing, near enough to pull me down before I cleared the trees. I was surrounded.

"So you did all this just to have a snack? The date? The restaurant? Why go to all the bother just to kill me. Couldn't you just kill humans instead?"

"Has your council truly stopped teaching you about us? How rich." Rachelle stepped from the darkness behind Shoshanna, and Mark followed suit.

"What do you want with me?"

"They are the King and Queen of the Artesian Pard. Show some respect," Sho answered for them.

"Show respect while they kill me? Not likely." My fists clenched, and I wracked my brain for an escape. There had to be a way out of this; there had to be.

Rachelle stepped forward and licked her lips. "I've waited for years for an Alori fledgling to break the Cardinal Laws and fall into my claws."

"Is that so, Rachelle?" We all turned to the south to see the Alori Council stepping from the shadows, flanked by their guard. "If your pard does not leave in the next ten seconds, the Alori Guard has full permission to kill on sight. Do you understand, Rachelle?"

Rachelle kept walking and didn't wait for an answer, growling through her teeth. "We could have killed him an hour ago, and yet here he stands. What makes you think we'd harm him?"

"Don't pretend. We know how you play with your food. Enough of your games. Leave, Rachelle. Now—and we may forgive the trespasses your Shoshanna made against our kind." The Counsel pointed at Sho standing behind her mother.

"She is guiltless. He broke the Law, and therefore is not protected under the treaty. We are within our rights!"

"Leave." As one, the Alori advanced a step.

Rachelle hissed but then rolled her shoulders, the last of her cat-like appearance disappearing between one moment and the next. "Consider this a declaration of war. Let's go everyone; we'll fight these birds another day."

The pard slipped into the brush, barely a whisper marking their passing.

The danger gone, I breathed in relief and reached toward my kinsflock. "I can't tell you how glad I am that you came looking for me. I thought I was dead. I've had enough of this human world. Let's go home."

Gabe stepped forward from the guard and put his hand on my chest not looking at me.

"You're not coming. You broke Cardinal Laws, and the council has decided this cannot go unpunished. Your choosing to disobey our most sacred laws is the key factor that has led us to war."

I looked between Gabe and the council members, deciding who to plead with. "Gabe, we're like brothers; please, help them see sense."

Tears rolled down his face. "Don't use our friendship against me, Jayson. Not now. I pleaded with you to be careful, but you chose this instead."

My stomach turned. "I'm sorry. Just give me another chance. Please? One more chance, and I swear I'll never mess up again."

Gabe faced the Counsel, and they whispered in low tones. Slowly, he turned back to me. "Jayson, for your breaking of the Cardinal Laws and the bringing of danger upon our flock, I hereby exile you." Gabe's voice wavered and a sob escaped him, but he pressed on. "If you attempt to come back the Guard will see you as an enemy of the flock and will exterminate you."

"No!" I dropped to my knees.

"You are allowed no goodbyes."

"Don't do this. Please." I begged, my shaking hands reaching for mercy.

His lips quivered. "It is already done. Farewell, Exiled One; may you find a way to overcome your sins."

They unfurled their wings as one and launched into the sky.

Numb, I watched them go—staring after their forms in the dark sky long after my eyes could no longer make them out. Movement caught my attention on the far side of the clearing: Shoshanna. A scream of rage ripped from my throat.

"You! I trusted you! I should kill you for what you've done, Shoshanna. You made me break Cardinal Law." I unfurled my wings and flew at her, slamming her against a tree. My fingers wrapped around her throat, crushing.

She narrowed her eyes and struggled against my hold. Her nails elongated into claws forcing my hand open. She gasped. "No. You made your own choices."

With a powerful thrust from my wings, I knocked her down, though the truth of her words stung. I knew the rules and I broke them. The choice was mine.

On the ground, she wiped her mouth with the back of her hand. "If it matters, I wish it could be different. That you and I—"

"Don't mock me. You made your choice as well. May the Dove bestow its curse upon you," I said in my native tongue. Shoshanna gasped, her eyes growing wide at the sounds of the sacred language, but I didn't stick around to hear any more protests or admissions of guilt from her. I took to the skies, an exiled Alori.

*The Alori shall never reveal their wings.*

*The Alori shall never speak the sacred tongue outside the Home.*

*The Alori shall never converse with a human except to secure provisions for the flock.*

# THE KEY TO A GOOD EDUCATION
## Gwendolyn McIntyre

*As you enter here, keep an open mind.*

In the center of the fountain in the central courtyard of the Kalen en Dar University, our world's only school of magic, stands a statue made of an unusual alloy that resists rust and oxidation.

The statue is that of a sorcerer, its eyes upraised in question and one hand pointing toward the haven of the gods. Around the base of the fountain are inscribed the words:

*The key to learning is to keep an open mind about all you might read, see, and hear, and to imagine the potential in all that is contained therein.*

This is the story of how the statue came to be.

**K**alen paused to make sure the parcel on his back was secure. He was late. Even with his peculiar night vision, it had taken him longer to descend the wall than planned. He'd needed to be careful in avoiding the darkened stones, magical artifacts placed in seemingly random locations in the walls. Contact with any one of them would have meant instant death.

Why so many people coveted the item he carried in his pack mystified him, but men had died trying to steal it. Admittedly, getting into the keep took hardly any effort. He'd expected the lower doors to be locked when the warlock departed on a trip to Royal City in the neighboring country and came prepared with the rope and a little judicious use of magic.

Gaining access to the inside of the tower had been easy, but disabling and bypassing the protections on the book had been harder than Kalen had anticipated, delaying him for hours while he observed each new trap with extra caution.

Once he secured the book in his pack, he turned to finding the key. Contrary to expectation, it wasn't on the hook where he usually saw it. Why Brindle had decided to take it with him tonight of all nights worried Kalen. He wondered if somehow Brindle expected the book to be taken.

It was well past sundown when he reached the base of the tower. He gave the rope a hard snap to release the hook caught high above. On the third try, it came free and fell toward the ground. With a small prayer of thanks to the god of thieves when it landed in the soft grass at the base of the tower, he spoke the words that caused it to shrink into a short piece the length of his arm. Stuffing it into his pack along with tonight's prize, he slipped through the shadows to where he'd left his horse.

Old and with a slow gait, Lumpkin wasn't the kind of horse a thief really needed, but the boy had grown fond of him.

"Once I'm paid for tonight's work, you're going to retire, old man." He rubbed the horse down and re-saddled him. "Though now we have business to see to."

Lumpy whickered, and Kalen patted his neck before swinging into the saddle. Turning toward the outskirts of town, the boy rolled in the saddle with Lumpy's lumbering gait. Hopefully, the client would be waiting at the designated meeting place; Kalen wanted to pass off *the item* as soon as he arrived.

Stealing the book from the tower had left him uneasy. Still, a job was a job.

**B**rindle en Dar, the kingdom's chief warlock, watched from the shadows inside the tower as the young man slipped away, then returned the object to the hook and spoke the words to dispel the illusion of himself walking away from the tower. The thief's stealth and efficiency impressed him. The young man had broken or sidestepped wards most experienced warlocks would have been at a loss to deal with.

Most remarkable was that he'd evaded the dancing stones, artifacts Brindle had built into his tower to deter unwelcome guests. With patience and careful observation, the boy discovered the pattern in the seemingly random movement of the dark stones.

Then again, given the young man was the son of a warlock and a sorceress, Brindle knew Kalen's actions would be purely instinctive. Brindle had expected his innate abilities would enhance his chosen profession, but he also thought the young man would fail. What would happen when training tempered the boy's raw talent?

He turned and put the kettle on the fire to heat. A cup of tea would help pass the time.

The cold iron of the bands around the book pressed hard into his back as Kalen dismounted and tied his horse to the post outside the gate. He could feel the potential of the magic inside of the book. What a shame he hadn't found the key, for it might have been interesting to read.

Just as well the client had offered a 'generous' reward, well above the agreed upon price for the book. He tired of worrying about where he'd live or when and what he'd eat. Best of all, there would be no more wondering who might be hunting him.

With a silly grin plastered on his face, he started through the gate, but a sodden thought made him stop. Being careless was a sure way to get himself killed. And considering his present client...

He stepped back and let his senses sweep the area. He thought for just a moment that no one hid in the shadows. The structure inside the gate and the out-building stood empty, but wait! There, in the corner. Someone squatted behind the sheltered entryway.

Unless his senses failed him, the kernel of untouchable life-magic in the figure was barely discernable, and yet a strong magical aura blazed around the figure. It confused him.

Choosing not to trust his magical sense, he bent down and picked up a few small pebbles. Stepping forward slowly, he pitched them one at a time onto the blind side of the shelter, getting closer to the corner with each throw. As the last one struck the edge of the hidden side, there came a shriek. A child ran out and tried to pass through the open gate.

Not knowing why he did it, Kalen grabbed the end of the magic rope and thought of a woven net strung between the gateposts, then threw it into the air. As it fell between the posts, the rope spun a web, infinitely stronger than one made by spiders.

It finished just as the child hit it at a run. Calling witch-light to himself, he noted with momentary surprise that his captive was a girl. She was perhaps no more than seven or eight years of age, with dirty blonde hair and bright golden green eyes. As the net wrapped around her and lowered her gently to the ground before releasing itself from the gate, he approached.

One moment she looked ready to scream, then the next she was stock-still and staring into his eyes. She spoke in a voice far older than the child she appeared to be.

"We beg you; do not give the sorcerer the book."

Surprised, he loosed the net from her and asked, "Why?"

She glanced back toward the gate before turning back to him. "He intends to use it for harm."

The girl smiled, reached out her small hand and touched him on the forehead. Kalen felt more than saw the brightness growing around her. When his sight returned, she was gone, but he remembered the words he thought she'd whispered in his ear.

*Save us.*

**H**e awoke in darkness, the child gone—if that was what she had been. Lumpy, still waiting where he'd been tied, gave his owner a disgruntled snort. With silent apologies, Kalen unsaddled the animal and left him to graze nearby.

The sound of an approaching rider interrupted his tasks. Globe lights, hanging from the wall lit themselves, announcing the presence of the sorcerer. Recognizing the pockmarked face of the tall, thin man who had hired him, he stood. He slipped the magic rope into one of his many hidden pockets.

"You're on time for a change," Fagos the sorcerer remarked as he dismounted, speaking something unintelligible to his horse before stepping toward the gate. "Come inside."

The sparse interior of the abode surprised Kalen—a complete change from the opulence of Brindle's massive tower. The entire single story building could have fitted into the first two floors of that structure.

It was apparent the man had few visitors with only two chairs in the front room. Both sat before a small table facing a fireplace. The exquisite collection in the library proved the Sorcerer had wealth. He appeared to favor a simple home and clothing, but it felt more like a disguise than a simple manner of taste.

Although he paid well, the man's presence made Kalen's skin crawl. The sooner he could complete the transaction and be on his way, the better.

He expected this meeting to be a repeat of their last one; the sorcerer giving orders and the thief asking questions, many of which had gone unanswered.

Brusque and to the point, his client demanded to see *the item*. Kalen removed his pack, slid the book out on the nearby table, and stepped away.

Fagos stepped forward to touch it, smiling as he did so, but then began to frown. He picked it up and turned it over, poking and prodding at it as if looking for a secret compartment.

Finally, he set it back down and turned on the younger man.

"What foolishness is this? This is nothing but an empty iron box. There is not even a keyhole."

Stepping forward, Kalen examined the book covered in brown dyed leather. Three hinged, cold-iron bands strapped into a long locking mechanism on the side of the book. Whatever had been written or printed on the cover was too faint, obscured by age, to be legible. Yet as he reached out and touched it, the book made a sound that to him seemed like a sigh of contentment. He turned to face the man.

"It is but an illusion. The lock," he placed a finger upon it, "is here. Once unlocked, the illusion will end."

"If that is so, then unlock it and allow me to examine it."

The thief shook his head. "That is a problem. The warlock, in his haste to attend elsewhere, took the key with him."

The sorcerer looked angry and suspicious. "You're certain of this."

Not a question, but instead an accusation.

"I watched him carefully. I know where he kept it, and I'd already discovered all of his hiding places. Unless there is a secret room with no door, it was not in his tower."

The man seemed to consider this for a moment. "The book is useless to me without the key, and for some reason, you can see past the illusion when I cannot. Therefore, you will make me a key."

The thief shook his head. "How? I don't know what the key is made of or how it needs to be shaped."

Scrupulous to never use magic in front of magicians, nor in sight of clients, lest it encourage them to use his magic for their own needs, Kalen shook his head. Job or no job, he would not harm a life with his magic, and according to rumors in the city, his current employer had no such qualms.

He looked up at the older man. "Can you not use magic to open it?"

The sorcerer turned red with rage, his reply more of a growl than speech. "One may not use magic to open the book, for to do so will destroy what is inside, which in turn will destroy the one trying to open it. You *will* find a way and make me a key. Now pick up the book."

Kalen barely had the book in his hands when the sorcerer shouted two words of command.

The thief felt as if he'd been shoved backwards into a bottomless pit. Oddly, as the world around him shifted, his concern was not for his own safety, but for whether the man would remember to feed Lumpkin in his absence.

The place Fagos had sent him looked very much like the shop belonging to his friend Ludej, the locksmith, except when he opened the door and stepped outside, he found himself in the same room he'd just exited. Turning the other way, he found a small room with a bed, a bathing room and a small cooking galley with an indoor hand-pump. The shop also housed a small kiln. A large quantity of the fuel necessary to fire it had been stockpiled by the door, as had bars and rods of every metal and alloy in the known world.

Kalen gave grudging admiration to the sorcerer for preparing so thoroughly for this possibility, sat down on the bed, and wondered aloud what he could do to save himself and the book.

*Click.*

The sound drew his eyes downward as the cover sprung open of its own volition. The book was handwritten, the pages far older than the cover that held them bound, the language ancient and obscure.

As he touched the page, Kalen felt something inside himself give way. He began to read.

*In later years, he would swear the book read itself to him.*

L ate the following day, Fagos arrived to see what progress had been made. What he saw confounded him. Kalen lay sleeping on the cot, his hands holding the book close to his chest, a smile upon his lips.

On the floor of the workroom lay many hundreds of keys. Each was similar in design save for the slight variations in the size of the bow and the shaping of the wards.

Picking up a handful, Fagos noted that they were made not just from the base metals and alloys he'd provided but also several new alloys. The thief, he decided, must have had some education or training in the arts of alchemy.

Attempting to kick a path clear, the sorcerer stepped forward to wake Kalen. To his surprise, the mere act of moving the keys caused an unexpected reaction. Instead of scattering, they stuck to his foot. Each step pulled more and more of them toward him until he was more than half covered with them. He staggered under the weight.

"What is this? What have you done?"

Angered, Fagos tried to dispel them using magic. Once again, the attempt backfired. Instead of falling away, the keys began to pull closer and closer together, as if they absorbed the energy from his magic. He could feel them drawing power, growing warm with stolen life.

Spells rolled off his tongue, but trying to draw the energy away from them only agitated the metal horde further, causing them to vibrate. They grew warmer with every passing second. He struggled as hot metal burned through his legging and seared his flesh beneath. A snarl ripped from his throat.

"No!"

I would stand very still and do nothing."

Face contorted in rage, the sorcerer stopped and looked up at Kalen sitting on the bed. The book lay in his lap. The trap had worked far better than he'd imagined, but the outcome was still a gamble, still in doubt.

"The key to understanding is to observe not simply actions but also inactions; to listen carefully not only to what is spoken, but also what is not."

As the sorcerer stopped fighting, several of the shaped artifacts fell away from him to pile near his feet.

He glared at Kalen. "Did you make one to open the book?"

The younger man smiled. "The key to understanding is to see things as they are, instead of as we wish them to be."

The sorcerer looked confused, but he snapped, "Answer my question."

Immediately, dozens more of the magical artifacts flew up from the ground and stuck to the ones already clinging to the sorcerer. The remainder of those already stuck to him singed his clothing. Wisps of smoke snaked up his body and circled overhead.

The thief stood, setting the book gently on the bed. "I had no need to make a key, for I had it with me all the time. I simply needed to recognize it for what it was."

"So you lied to me!"

"No, I listened to the book."

The older man raised an arm, and Kalen shook his head. He didn't want a death on his hands, even if it was this wretch who passed for a magic-user. "The heat you feel is caused by the metal alloys leaching the heat and energy from your body. The more you struggle, the more magic you use, all the more they will draw from you."

Shocked into inaction, the man glared at Kalen, but his voice was calm as he spoke. "You opened it?"

He nodded. "Interesting what you can learn from a good book."

Ignoring the warning, the sorcerer drew power to himself. "You will die for your impudence!"

"No!" Kalen held out his hand. "You don't understand what you're doing!"

Even if he had cared to listen to Kalen, it was too late. The surge of magic pulled the remainder of the artifacts up off the floor to cover the man, leaching away the power and transforming it into heat so rapidly that the keys melted almost instantly.

Kalen covered his ears to drown out the scream.

As if it were sentient, the molten metal began to flow over and down the sorcerer, engulfing him. Within minutes a metal statue of the sorcerer stood in the centre of the room.

Kalen picked up the book. "Time to go home."

With the sorcerer's death, the spell that had kept Kalen captive broke. As he stepped out through the open door, he found himself exiting one of the outbuildings behind the house.

Returning to Fagos's quarters, he hunted until he found the room where the sorcerer had chained stolen children and locked them in as slaves. He searched their faces, seeking the girl he'd seen before. She had to be here—she had to be.

In the darkest corner, a little bed cradled a silent form chained to its frame. She'd been dead for several days. He covered her and bowed his head, remembering the intelligence in the eyes of the bright spirit he'd met just the day before.

Eyes tearing, he released the rest of the children, and with a promise to return quickly, he rode for help.

Barely an hour later, he returned with the law-keepers, a priest, and a wagon to carry the children. The priest promised that the rest of the children would be returned to their families, and though no one knew her name, the girl would receive a proper burial. Kalen couldn't help but feel that he'd failed her, but the knowledge that the others would be cared for helped ease his soul.

The sorcerer's home was, by law, forfeit to Kalen.

With his new house in order, Kalen and Lumpy headed back into the city. As he rode toward the warlock's tower, he thought on the horrors that Fagos had committed and decided to move the sorcerer to a prominent place in the courtyard as a reminder to anyone tempted to use magic against the innocent that such cruelty never went unpunished.

**B**rindle and his wife watched as Kalen replaced the book carefully, almost reverently, from where he had taken it, then turned to face the couple.

"I am sorry, Father, Mother. I expect you'll not wish me to live here. You'll not want a thief in your house."

Brindle shook his head, but it was Kalen's mother who spoke.

"You carry our love, hopes, and dreams with you all the time. You simply need to recognize your immeasurable worth for what it is."

The couple enveloped Kalen in an embrace. His father smiled.

"Welcome home, son."

# THE BOOKSELLER
## Katrina Monroe

*It's only a summer job, but the mystery
held inside a book reveals other plans.*

Erin tapped her foot on the tile floor, shifted her weight, and then checked the clock. Again. Six thirty and Angus still hadn't shown up. The trickle of customers had come and gone, leaving $75.67 as the only sign that they'd been there. The downtown pedestrian traffic had increased with restaurant goers, street-corner musicians and the occasional vagabond. Most passed by the Book Bin as though it didn't exist.

Closing time ticked closer. Erin held the number of a former employee, Chloe, in one hand, and her cell in the other. Her new boss, Angus, hadn't left a number. She started to dial, then shoved the phone in her back pocket. *Not yet.* Chloe had said Angus was unpredictable; maybe he would show up just in time to count the meager till and send Erin on her way. She fixed her eyes on the door, anticipating the moment when he would come hobbling in on his knotty wooden cane, his mouth pursed and puckered in his perusal. But the moment never came. At six fifty-five, she dialed Chloe's number.

"Hello?"

"Chloe, its Erin."

"Oh. Hi. What's up?"

"Well, Angus hasn't shown up yet and I'm not sure what to do."

"That doesn't surprise me. He does that from time to time."

"Okay, so, what should I do? Is there a key or something for the front door?"

"Um, yea. It will either be taped underneath the register or on the front table on the mezzanine."

Erin slid her long fingers in the space between the register and the counter. No key. "It's not under the register."

"Upstairs, then."

"But, I thought we weren't supposed to—"

"Well, serves him right for not showing up on your first day. If he comes back giving you hell, then tell him you'll take your case to the union.

Don't know that there is a bookseller's union, but it always got him to can it when I couldn't get him off my back."

"Okay..."

"And don't worry about the register," Chloe continued. "When he comes in, he will do the paperwork for it. I made the mistake of trying to help one time, and he spent the next three days trying to find some kind of mistake in my math. He accused me of stealing fifty-three cents from him."

*What have I gotten myself into?* "I'll just lock the door then. Thanks Chloe."

Chloe hung up without saying goodbye.

Erin took one last look at the front door and sighed. She remembered his words clearly: *You go in my office, you'll be out on your bum faster'n you can say 'God save the Queen.'*

She gingerly lifted the register again to make sure she hadn't missed the key the first time. No key. She traced her fingers on the underside of the counter, and jerked her hand back when her fingers traced over someone's ancient, dried gum. She wiped her hand on her jeans and eyed the staircase—a guillotine—and she, Marie Antoinette. Fired.

The creaking of the decrepit beams under Erin's feet were louder than before, like a squealing alarm.

"Key. Chloe told me to." She pointed to the front door, over enunciating for the benefit of the video camera she wasn't sure even existed.

She paused on every other step to check over her shoulder, certain she heard the sleigh bells on the door, and finally reached the top of the stairs. A short end table hugged against the mezzanine railing. The deep, green paint flaked off the legs like curled crayon shavings. With a little wiggling, she opened the single drawer. Save for a few mothballs, it was empty.

*Damn it.* She shoved her hand to the back of the drawer and felt around. No key.

She shut the drawer, mumbled a half-hearted *Abracadabra*, then opened it again.

Of course, it hadn't appeared. *Worth a shot.*

She looked on the floor under the table, then walked a two foot perimeter around the table, scanning the floor, plank by plank. Somewhere between analyzing the circular grain in the wood and cursing the entire western hemisphere because without a job to pay for insurance, she couldn't keep the car her parents gave her as a sixteenth birthday present, a faint glow from underneath the office door caught Erin's eye. *What in the world?*

She opened the door slowly, trying to minimize the squeal from the hinges. The chaos covering the top of Angus's desk made it impossible to tell if the key hid somewhere in the mix. Erin settled into his chair, careful to stay on the edge so she wouldn't disrupt the shifted padding, and, afraid to move anything, visually sifted through the piles.

After going over the desk twice, she still hadn't found it. She slid each of the six drawers open, one by one. All empty except the last, which had only a dried sprig of mistletoe tucked into the back of it.

Erin fell into an exasperated heap on the floor and sat, legs crossed, with her elbows on her knees and her face in her hands. The way she saw it, she now had three choices.

One: leave the Book Bin, unlocked, and pray nothing was stolen by morning; or two: sleep behind the counter all night; or three: pester Chloe again and likely get hung up on. She wanted nothing to do with any of those.

*It has to be here. It just has to.*

The only other piece of furniture in the office was a bookshelf, covered with intricate carvings and filled with a mix of volumes, both old and new.

Erin decided to pull the books down one at a time starting at eye level. She reached up and took hold of the soft spine of a book called *Unlocked*. As she slid the book off the shelf, a thunderous, reverberating boom like a tumbler engaging in a giant combination lock punched through the room. The vibration rocked through her body, and she staggered backward into the desk. Her fall knocked the piles on the corner of the desk to the ground, scattering paper, notebooks, and all manner of odds and ends across the floor. She took deep, labored breaths to calm her heart as it jack-hammered in her chest.

"Keeper," the dark, raspy voice of a woman echoed around her followed by the sound of hundreds of flapping wings.

A scream froze in Erin's throat, and out of the corner of her eye, she spotted a glint of shiny metal. The key. Caring only for escape, she stumbled toward the key, barely able to grasp it before running from the room. A menacing chuckle followed her as she nearly tumbled down the stairs and out the front door.

Hugh Kellen hated hospitals. No, he loathed them. Here he sat in the same waiting room, assaulted by the overwhelming aroma of the antibacterial stuff. It smelled like poison permeating the atmosphere. He knew it was slowly eating away at the hairs inside his nose and ripping at his lungs.

He hated the nurses, dressed in their happy little scrubs with pink hearts and cartoon animals dancing across their broad asses. He knew their secret: Clipboard-carrying angels of death—so sorry there isn't anything else they can do.

He watched the yuppie sitting across from him gingerly sipping his steaming cup of what purported to be coffee. It brought to Hugh's mind the insect-infested ponds of his youth that dappled the countryside like freckles on the face of Eire. Hugh was smugly satisfied at the grimace spreading across the yuppie's face as the mud

197

oozed into his mouth. *A ray of sunshine in this dismal place.*

Hugh had woken with the sun and headed to the hospital to see Angus, his best friend, hoping with enough verbal abuse, he could coax the old man out of his own head. The doctor called it a coma, but Hugh knew better... nothing more than stubborn-arse syndrome. Angus Davey was a fighter and would never give in to something as unproductive as a coma. But, Hugh also knew Angus was tired. A series of heart attacks and subsequent surgeries had left Angus only half himself—slow moving and quiet—but still a stubborn arse. Hugh arrived a little over an hour before visiting hours in the ICU, so he was stuck in the waiting room, mere feet from Angus's room, until the stethoscope-wearing Gestapo behind the desk would let him in.

Catching his own reflection in the gleaming stainless-steel counter at the front of the waiting room, he ran his calloused and scarred fingers through the thinning gray on his head. Father Time had not been kind to him. Only fifty-eight years old, but looked seventy and felt eighty. His once piercing eyes faded to a dirty gray, and deep lines etched into his forehead, carved from decades of intense thought and worry. He looked away from the old man in the reflection to see the yuppie walking away, leaving his full cup of mud next to a plant. The burnt stale aroma clung to the air, almost as strong as the disinfectant pall. Almost.

Hugh pushed back the sleeve of his windbreaker and looked at his watch. Seven fifty-nine. He stood slowly, allowing his creaking bones to adjust themselves for walking. He took one step before a horde of scrubs came running from all directions toward Angus's room, one of them pushing a crash cart. Panic-stricken, he braced himself on the back of a chair. Angus had always been the stronger one, a thousand times more resilient than Hugh.

This wasn't right. This couldn't be happening.

"What's going on?" he yelled, but no one answered. The nurses behind the counter, on the phone, turned their backs to him, and the others had run to Angus's room without stopping. *Hold on, Gus! Sweet Mother Mary, hold on!*

A shroud descended on Hugh, making it difficult to see and breathe. He found himself alternating between holding his breath as if to block out the reality of what had happened and hyperventilating. Like looking through a gauze filter, making everything dim and blurry, he struggled in a sea of surreal. Angus dead? Couldn't be.

The nurse sat beside him, placed a gentle hand on his knee, and told him there was nothing they could do. He'd heard her voice, felt her hand, and held the weighty stack of paperwork. But it wasn't real.

He drove home on auto-pilot, signaling, responding to changes in traffic, stopping when he should, and maintaining a safe speed throughout the whole trip, but he didn't remember any of it. Surprised to find himself at home, he stared at the dark windows from his driveway, not sure he wanted to be there. He rested his forehead against the steering wheel for a moment before forcing his hand to open the car door and his legs to swing to the ground. Slowly, he heaved himself up and walked to the house—a far older man than when he'd left this morning.

Memories of his friend slammed into him as he stepped over the threshold. Sharing Chinese take-out at his table, laughing over card games, cheering for their favorite soccer team on TV, crying together as they picked out Hugh's wife's funeral dress… Another death, and this time, he faced it alone.

Angus had no family, so the burden of arrangements for the funeral and for getting his affairs in order fell to Hugh, as directed by his old friend's will. They'd spoken about it after Angus's first heart attack. But Hugh never thought he would have to think about it again. Angus had sworn out loud one day he would live forever, and Hugh had believed him.

But they both had been wrong.

He sifted through the papers the hospital gave him. Among them, he found a copy of Angus's living will the attorney left with the hospital staff when Angus had slipped into the coma. An envelope lay on top of the stack, "To be opened upon my death" written across the front in spidery, angular hand.

At first, Hugh just stared at it. Opening it would acknowledge that his best friend, his cohort, his brother, was truly gone. The unopened letter taunted him from the coffee table. Hugh wanted to tear it to bits, then throw it into a roaring fire and bury the ashes. But instead, after turning it over and over, putting it down and picking it back up several times, he peeled the flap open and pulled the pages out. He unfolded the lined paper and began to read Angus's scribbled handwriting.

*Hugh,*

*If you're reading this, then... well, I've gone from this God-forsaken earth. About time, too, if you ask me. Here I am writing this, a man of fifty, but I feel centuries old. But then, I suppose I am.*

*You've been like a brother to me, but I have to put on you a burden—one that you don't deserve, but since I'm not there... You need to prepare my replacement for me. I don't know who they are. All I know is how to find them.*

*For as far back as the books tell us, a group of teachers and philosophers in Ireland called Druids searched for someone. Someone, a keeper, who held the deep magic of Nature. The triskele. This person would entomb a malevolent triple-goddess called the Morrigan.*

*A raven in her most powerful form, the Morrigan has threatened me for years, promising me that when I fail to find my replacement, she will rise and consume everything, everyone, and cover the world in darkness.*

*This cannot happen!*

*I am a Keeper. As long as I live the Morrigan remains entombed. I have been her jailer for twenty years, three months, and twenty-one days, searching for my replacement so when I pass, it can continue to be guarded. The magic that binds her will only last a few days after my death unless you find a new keeper. She will try to stop you; I know she will.*

*Hugh, find my apprentice. If I am dead, then the power is already within Morrigan's reach. Her lust for devastation will drive her to destroy everything without prejudice.*

*The power is real, as well as the danger it holds. If my apprentice isn't worthy, if the magic of my people isn't present in them, the power will kill them when invoked. Years ago, I set up a system, a locked puzzle of sorts, to lead my apprentice to the grove, with precautions taken so only my true apprentice will be able to sort through it and reach it. They will find the path on their own. Their deep-seated instincts will lead them to the key, but they will need your guidance. They won't believe. You*

*will have to push them toward it. I don't know
how long you will have.*

*My bookstore hides the key. Wait there for my
replacement. They will come. They have to.*

*Angus*


Hugh wiped his sweaty palms on his pants,
clutching Angus's letter. He turned his head
toward the window. The oppressive clouds hung
low, and he couldn't shake the feeling that
something had changed while he'd been reading.

**E**rin's jeans were no protection against the
cold concrete curb. The day after "The
Incident," she forced herself to go back to
work at the Book Bin. She couldn't explain it, but
she felt as though she had to. But the feeling only
pushed her as far as the shop door.

It was the old man who got her to go inside.

He strode past her, didn't even seem to notice
her presence, and unlocked the door. Confused,

Erin leapt to her feet and followed the man inside. As soon as the door closed behind her, a pressing heaviness surrounded her.

"Where did you get that key?"

The man spun around, startled. "Who are you?" He shook his head and didn't wait for an answer. "We aren't opening today."

She took a step backward. "I work here. Angus hired me."

At the mention of Angus's name, the man cringed. "Well, I won't need you today. You can just go home."

Both relieved to be leaving the store—which was giving her the creeps the longer she stayed— and confused as to who this man was, giving her orders, Erin started for the door.

She heard a sigh and hurried footsteps behind her. "Wait," the man said.

One hand on the door, Erin turned toward him, cringing.

"Do you…" Eyebrows knitted, his eyes fixed on the floor. Erin could almost read the internal battle on his face. "Does the term, 'Keeper,' mean anything to you?"

Heat filled Erin's chest. Keeper. That's what the voice had called her, wasn't it? She studied his face for a moment. "No," she finally answered.

His face fell, then became hard. "Nevermind."

"I'm Erin," she said, offering a shaky hand.

After a moment's hesitation, he took it. "Hugh." He looked around the store then asked, "You wouldn't know where Angus kept his paperwork, would you?"

The past tense of the statement didn't escape Erin's notice. The stiffness of his stance didn't invite any questions so she asked none. Besides, having to show Hugh the room where she'd heard the voice filled her with dread.

"Upstairs. There's an office on the mezzanine."

Hugh gestured to the staircase. "Ladies, first."

Reluctantly, Erin walked to the stairs and started up. Knowing that Hugh was behind her did little to comfort her. She could feel that something was…off. Stopping at the top of the stairs, she stood sideways so Hugh could walk past her. Erin braced herself against the railing at the top step and held her breath as he unlocked the office door. The hinge creaked open.

Silence, interrupted only by the sound of paper being scuffed against the floor.

After a long exhale, Erin crept toward the office and peered around the door jam. A floorboard squealed under her feet; Hugh looked up.

"What happened here?" He pointed to the desk.

Erin shrugged, not looking at him or the desk. *He wouldn't believe me anyway.*

Her muscles were tight—prepared to run. The creaking of the floorboards under Hugh as he walked around the desk sent shivers up her spine. The voices were here. She could feel it. The sound of feathers rustling against the wood of the bookshelf interrupted the silence. Her gut clenched; she wanted to throw up and scream at the same time.

Hugh sighed, and began shifting stacks of paper to the floor on top of the scattered mess. It looked like a hurricane had come through. Paper covered the floor, and the chair behind the desk rested on its side. But, what caught Erin's attention was the book. *Unlocked.* She was sure she'd dropped it on the ground before running out. Now, it stood, alone, against the side of the top shelf.

A shudder pulsed through her. Hugh looked up from his task again and followed Erin's stare to the book.

He walked toward the shelf and reached out to grab it. "This important?"

"No!" Erin ran into the room, nearly bowling Hugh over in her desperate attempt to get between him and the book. "Please..."

He paused, his arm still extended. "Why?"

She opened her mouth, but nothing came out at first. "You wouldn't believe me."

Hugh stared at her for a long time, but Erin couldn't read his expression. He probably thought she was crazy. He reached into his jacket, pulling out a folded piece of paper, examined it for a long minute, and handed it to Erin. "Read this."

She hesitated but accepted it.

Hugh stared at her expectantly. "Go on."

Erin opened the paper, and as she did so, *Unlocked* fell from the shelf.

They both froze.

Hugh jabbed the paper with his finger. "Read."

"But, I—"

"Read."

Erin did as she was told and Hugh retrieved the book.

*Morrigan.* Something primal deep in her clicked when she read the word. She didn't know what it was, who they were, but she knew she was terrified. Could they—she—be the voices? What did it have to do with her? They called her 'Keeper.' *Keeper of what? Surely they can't mean me?*

She looked up from the letter just as he opened the cover.

"I don't understand…" She turned the letter over in her hands.

"I don't either." He pulled a yellowing paper from the front of the book and handed it to Erin. "Careful. It looks delicate."

A map. At the bottom left corner was a symbol, a three-armed shape with a swirl at the end of each arm. The longer she looked at it, the stranger she felt. She couldn't shake the feeling that she had seen it somewhere. Erin searched her memory to the limit but found nothing. Her eyes moved across the map, taking in as much as possible, but she couldn't grasp its meaning.

"Where is this place?"

"Eire. Ireland."

"How do you –"

"I'd know it anywhere..." Hugh glanced wistfully over the map. "It was my home. Angus's home. This is where we grew up." Then, his eyes fixed on a point on it and grew wide. "Look." He pointed to a green smudge.

Erin squinted to read the slanted handwriting. "Nemeton?"

"Maybe he wasn't crazy. Maybe..." he murmured. Suddenly, Hugh started for the door.

Erin panicked. "Wait! Where are you going?"

"Stay here."

She stood, frozen, clutching the map. What was happening? Why did she feel this way?

Hugh burst through the doorway, carrying another book. He threw it onto the desk and furiously turned the pages. Snatching the map out of her hand, Hugh pointed to the green smudge again. "Nemeton. It's a real place. Look. Killarney National Park. They're the same place."

"And?" Erin's hands shook.

"And I don't know why I'm even saying this, but I think... I think you need to go there."

Before the thought fully processed in her mind, Erin said, "I think so, too."

Hugh offered *Unlocked* to Erin, "And I think you should take this with you."

She accepted the book, and the moment the cover touched her fingers, the light was sucked from the room, leaving Erin in blackness. She reached out to Hugh, but she only felt the empty air.

"Hugh?"

It was like she was in a vacuum. The sound dissipated instantly.

She felt feathers brush her cheek. She fell to her knees, shivering, with her arms wrapped tightly around herself. Panic seized her chest and she couldn't breathe. *They're going to kill me.*

She waited. Then, she smelled something unusual. It was impossible to ignore. *Dirt? Trees? Where am I?*

Too scared to open her eyes, she reached down. Grass.

*Open your eyes. If you can't see them coming, you can't run. You're a sitting duck. On the count of three. One… Two…*

She forced her eyes open.

A forest, deep and dense, stood sentry around her. She knelt at the center of a clearing, alone. On the grass in front of her, the book opened to a page near the center. Scribbled in the margin in the same handwriting as the letter, was a note:

*Welcome home.*

Suddenly, fragments of memories flashed in her head. They weren't hers, but she could see them as clearly as if she had been there.

Three women. A man stood over them. He said something. Erin strained to hear, though she knew it was impossible. The women shimmered. A penetrating light, and then she saw it as vividly as if it stood in front of her now.

A raven where the women once stood. It raised its black wings and flew at the man, digging its claws into his face. Erin screamed and threw her hands up to protect herself.

The memory jumped. The clearing where she now knelt. Three men; one with a long, white beard, barely able to walk, and the other two leading him by the arms.

The old man, white scars slashed across his face, turned and looked at her. Not past her, as though looking at something in the memory, but at her. She felt the weight of his stare. He turned away, slowly, and she watched his every move. His arms in the air. The raven appeared and Erin suppressed a shudder. Still no sound, but she was sure he said something. *Tell me. Please tell me.*

He raised his hands and moved his mouth in silent speech. Erin raised hers as well. Welling up from her gut, burning through her chest, words poured from her mouth in a language she didn't understand. And yet, the words felt right and good.

A blinding light flashed in her mind, and Erin shut her eyes on impulse. When it subsided, the raven was gone, and in its place, three black-haired women. The same from the first vision. A white ball of light burst from the woman in the center and flew into one of the young men, melting into his chest. *Into her chest.* He glowed with strength and power, and when she looked down, she could see the brightness of her own skin. The power inside her thrummed in unison with the beating of her heart.

The Raven Women sank into the ground, screaming and clutching at the grass. Then the vision ended.

Still on her knees, Erin ran her fingers through the blades of grass. She could feel them pulsing on her fingertips, as though each individual blade had a heartbeat. She dug her nails into the dirt and felt a vibration. She wasn't afraid.

She gazed upward. A breeze rustled the top limbs and flowed down to her, whipping her hair. "It'll be okay. I'm here."

# HER FATHER'S EYES
## S. M. Carrière

*Grandmother holds the key to the past...*
*and future.*

**W**hat is it, Grandma?" Rowena asked. The old-fashion key, rusted now with age, felt solid and heavy in her palm.

"It's a key, dear."

"Thank you, I figured that much out myself," Rowena grumbled.

"The truth is I don't know what it's for. It's very old though. My grandmother gave it to me on my sixteenth birthday, and she got it from her grandmother and so on down the line through lord knows how many generations. I've tried it on every door on the property. It never worked. But it must be important. We never keep anything unless it's important. I can't think of a better present for you."

"Right," Rowena drawled. "Uh, thanks, Grandma."

"You're welcome, dear; now run upstairs and finish your homework while I make your birthday dinner."

Rowena turned and bolted up the stairs to her room, slamming the door a good deal harder than she ought, and tossed the key on her dresser.

Most normal girls would be having a huge birthday party. They'd have mountains of presents, all of them cool, like an iPod or a diamond necklace.

Not Rowena, no. She had lived with her grandmother for as long as she could remember. Her mother had disappeared shortly after Rowena was born, and Rowena had no idea where her mother and father were. There were no photos of either of them about the house.

As a result, Rowena had to spend her birthday doing homework and eating dinner with her grandmother, whose only gift was an old, useless, piece-of-junk key. Rowena kicked her school book and sat heavily on her bed.

It wasn't her grandmother's fault. Old people are strange. Her grandmother was stranger than most, and, according to her classmates at the all-girl grammar school she attended, so was she.

Rowena took up a brush and combed out her raven hair. The brush cast sparkles in the lamplight, reflecting back to her in the mirror. She wasn't really sure what made her so different from everyone else at school, but she certainly felt different.

Rowena set the brush aside and picked up her biology textbook. She barely had time to open it when her grandmother called to her from the kitchen.

"Rowena! Dinner's ready!"

Rowena shut the book and thumped down the stairs. It smelled wonderful in the kitchen. Her grandmother had cooked lamb, her specialty and Rowena's favorite. They ate in silence. Rowena bit her lip and tried to stifle her hopes for more birthday gifts though her grandmother seemed quite content to eat in silence. When dinner was done, Rowena bolted up the stairs again to start on her homework while her grandmother tidied up the kitchen, humming to herself.

Around ten o'clock, Rowena finally crawled between the sheets of her bed. There was a soft knock at the door.

"Yes?"

Her grandmother opened it and bustled in with a tray laden with a jug of cold milk and honey and a small plate of biscuits. "Rowena, dear, would you like some milk and biscuits?"

Rowena sat up and smiled. "Yes please."

"Here you are, love," her grandmother said. She placed the tray on Rowena's lap and poured a glass of milk. "My mother used to give me milk and cookies before I went to bed every night and then sing me to sleep. I always had such lovely dreams after."

Rowena smiled at her grandmother. "Did you sing my mother to sleep?"

"Of course I did. That's what I'm here for," her grandmother replied. She reached out and stroked Rowena's straight hair wistfully. "You can tell that you are a Fae. All that straight black hair. You look just like her."

"Like who? Mother?"

Her grandmother nodded. Rowena bit back the question she had asked a thousand times over. There was no point in asking why her mother left her. Her grandmother never answered with anything but "I don't know, love."

Rowena finished her milk and biscuits. "Thank you."

"You're welcome, dear. Would you like anything else?"

Rowena shook her head, and her grandmother picked up the tray and started for the door.

"Actually..."

Her grandmother turned and raised her brows.

"Would you sing me to sleep?"

Her grandmother's smile could have lit the night sky. She put down the tray on the nightstand and sat beside Rowena, ensuring she was well wrapped in blankets and began to sing.

*Hush, my love,*
*Sleep, my love.*
*Lady Night keeps watch,*
*Raiment of stars about her.*
*Hush. Sleep.*

*Hush, my love,*
*Sleep, my love.*
*Mistress Dream sings sweet,*
*Riding high upon the wind-horse.*
*Hush. Sleep.*

*Hush, my love,*
*Sleep, my love.*
*Lord Dark will not find thee,*
*For Lady Moon surrounds thee.*
*Hush. Sleep.*

Her grandmother smiled gently and kissed Rowena's brow. "It never fails," she said, before picking up the tray and leaving Rowena to sleep. Rowena smiled to herself.

**R**owena did not want to get out of bed. It took a great deal of her grandmother's cheerful cajoling to get Rowena to put her feet on the floor and get dressed. Her grandmother left to prepare breakfast. Late, as usual, Rowena threw on a pair of jeans and a crumpled shirt, chucked books haphazardly into her backpack, and wrenched open her bedroom door.

*Rowena.*

She turned to find the room empty and in its usual state. Nary a curtain rustled. Her gaze fell across the key that lay on her vanity top. She grabbed it before rushing out the door and down the stairs to the kitchen, putting the soft, breathy voice out of her mind.

"Rowena!" her grandmother greeted as she came through the kitchen door. Rowena grabbed the buttered toast from the plate her grandmother held and donned her red coat.

"I'm late." She dashed out the door.

"Have a good day, dear!" her grandmother called. If Rowena had heard, it didn't show. She grabbed her bike, a vintage thing so rusted it was likely to fall apart any moment, and jumped on.

It began to drizzle.

"Perfect. Just perfect," Rowena muttered darkly as she cycled up the hill.

Though one of the most prestigious schools in the town, she loathed almost everything about Cartier Girl's Grammar. Its posh façade, its ludicrous old-style buildings, built just twenty years ago, and the fact that all the teachers seemed to detest her. She especially hated her fellow students; perfect, pretentious blonde angels with their noses in the air, who turned into vicious harpies the moment a teacher's back was turned.

Rowena did love one thing about school, and that was her weekly forty-five minute music lessons. She was learning the lever harp and was certain that no instrument in the world could ever sound so beautiful.

Today was Thursday, and that meant two things; English class, which she despised, and her music lesson.

The rain grew steadily harder as the day wore on. Rowena stared out the window for almost every class and paid little attention to the teachers' lectures.

In English class, Ms. Rose droned in an unwavering monotone about Shakespeare as Rowena's attention drifted outside once more.

"...has become the biggest problem. Rowena? Rowena, are you listening to me? Rowena Fae!"

Rowena snapped around. "It looks like there will be a storm this afternoon."

"What?"

"It...I'm sorry, Miss Rose, what were you saying?"

"Heavens, girl! You are the most difficult student I've ever had to deal with!"

*I'm not like the other girls. I never have been like them.*

Immediately following lunch, Mr. Westworth taught her music lessons. His gentle encouragement had made Rowena a fine harp player. Though elderly, he surely must have been very handsome in his youth, with eyes as green as spring grass—sparkling like dew in the morning sun—and a wide smile. He greeted her at the door of the music room with a towel, having spied her approaching in the pouring rain with nothing but her coat to shield her.

"Do you not own an umbrella, Miss Fae?" he asked her as she removed her coat and toweled off.

"I forgot it."

"Hmph. Make sure your hands are dry. I don't want these strings getting wet."

"Yes, Mr. Westworth."

Rowena sat at the harp, and Mr. Westworth opened the music book. "Right, what would you like to play?"

"Planxty Lady Wrixon."

Mr. Westworth smiled. "One of my favorites." He flipped the pages, and Rowena began to play. As always, she became lost in her music and did not notice a beautiful sound emanating from her coat pocket until Mr. Westworth shifted. She stopped, and the sound, like singing crystal, died away.

Frowning, Rowena rose from her seat and went to her coat. She fished out the ancient key. It did not look any different.

"What is that?" asked Mr. Westworth.

"A key. My grandmother gave it to me for my birthday yesterday."

"Well, Happy Birthday." He smiled warmly.

"Thanks."

"What's it for?"

"I don't know. Neither does Grandma."

"May I?" Mr. Westworth held out his hand, and Rowena placed the key on it. He put it up to the light and examined it from all angles. "Well, it doesn't seem that special. Very old, yes, but not that special."

"It can't have been the thing that made that noise." Rowena frowned.

"Let's experiment, shall we?" Mr. Westworth placed the key on a side table and went to the harp. He began to play. Both he and Rowena watched the key carefully. It did nothing.

"Hmm." He sounded disappointed.

"Let me try."

Mr. Westworth gave her the seat and Rowena began to play. Not one bar into her Planxty, the key started to sing, the sound clear and high and sweet.

"Oh my!" Mr. Westworth breathed.

"I don't believe it!"

A rapid knock at the door brought them both back from their intense study of the key. "Mr. Westworth?"

Mr. Westworth snatched up the key as he called, "Just a minute." He pressed the key into Rowena's hand. "I do not know what this is for. But it's very special. Keep it close."

She nodded and hurriedly put on her coat. "Thank you, Mr. Westworth."

"No, no, my girl. Thank you."

With her mind awhirl, Rowena stepped out of the music room and ran to her next class in the pouring rain.

The rain did not let up for the rest of the day. By the time school ended, the thunder and lightning started. Rowena cursed savagely as she pedaled home in the downpour. The sky had grown dark, as if it were evening already. She arrived at the front door of her tiny house just as lightning struck immediately above and barged inside as the thunder shook the house.

"Heavens to Betsy!" her grandmother exclaimed as Rowena stumbled in. "You look like a drowned rat!"

"Thanks," Rowena mumbled.

"Come inside, child, and shut that door. I'll fetch you a towel."

Soaking wet and cold, Rowena did as she was bid. She shivered in the tiny foyer until her grandmother bustled back from the linen cupboard with an armload of towels.

"I only need one, Grandma." She smiled gratefully nevertheless.

"That's what you think. You're still swimming. Now, off with your jacket and shoes."

Rowena removed her jacket, and her grandmother threw a towel around her shoulders. "Come on in. I'll run you a hot bath and make some tea. That should warm you up."

Rowena nodded and allowed her grandmother to fuss over her. It was not long until she found herself in the tub, surrounded by suds that smelled sweetly of strawberry and jasmine.

Her grandmother carried in a tray of chamomile tea.

"Here you are, love. Nothing soothes the body like a nice, hot cuppa." She poured the cup and handed it to Rowena, who took it and relaxed into the warm water. Despite the storm thrashing like a wounded dragon outside, inside this house, in the presence of her grandmother, Rowena felt safe and happy. How could her mother have wanted anything else? She lowered the cup from her lips without taking a sip.

"Grandma?"

"Yes, dear?"

"Why did mother leave me?"

"I don't know, love, but it was very wrong of her."

Rowena frowned. That was not the usual response. Her grandmother's tone sounded sharper than usual, angrier than the softly spoken, often sad responses of the past.

"What is it, dear?" her grandmother asked.

"Nothing." She once again raised the teacup to her lips.

*Don't!*

A strange voice shrieked from downstairs, ringing like crystal. Rowena's head snapped up, and she looked at her grandmother. "Did you hear that?"

"Hear what, love?"

"That voice."

"What voice, dear?"

"Nothing, never mind. Must've just been the house shaking. Do you mind if I just soak a bit?"

"Of course, dear. Oh, silly me, hanging around in the washroom! Drink your tea and come downstairs when you're ready. I'll put some supper on the table."

"Thanks, Grandma."

Her grandmother left the bathroom, humming an unfamiliar tune. Rowena's scowl deepened.

"Hello?" Rowena whispered to the empty air once her grandmother was out of sight. There was no response. "Rowena Fae, you have lost your mind," she scolded herself. She raised the cup once again.

*No! Run!* came the shriek once more.

"What?" Rowena whispered.

*Run, Rowena! Run!*

Gasping, she jumped out of the tub, spilling her tea in the water. Her heart racing, she toweled off and ran into her room and threw on whatever clothes her hands touched.

Hearing her grandmother in the kitchen humming her strange song and clanging about noisily, Rowena crept as quietly as she could down the stairs to the door. She had only just reached for her coat when she heard her name. She turned and faced her grandmother, who stood at the kitchen doorway, draped in light but looking dark.

"Where are you going, Rowena? You didn't drink your tea," her grandmother asked. The voice Rowena heard did not belong to her grandmother.

"I…I forgot something…at school," Rowena managed to stutter. "It's important. I have to go back and get it." She pulled her coat off the rack and struggled into it.

"No. You aren't going anywhere." Her grandmother drifted towards the door. Her toes dragged on the floor as she glided forward, her eyes blank and dark.

Rowena screamed. She turned, flung open the door, and raced out into the storm, coat in hand. She dared look over her shoulder only once, and through the haze of tears, she saw the lifeless form of her grandmother gliding after her, eyes boring into the back of her.

Running blind, Rowena mustered what strength she could and ran to the only place her feet knew where to go, Cartier Girl's Grammar.

Her grandmother, or what used to be her grandmother, still in pursuit, Rowena ran full long onto the campus. She rounded the corner of the Arts Building and collided with something—something that let out a winded "harrumph" and spilled papers everywhere. Rowena screamed again as long, strong fingers wrapped around her arms.

"Rowena!" a familiar voice exclaimed.

Rowena looked up into the sparkling green eyes of Mr. Westworth.

"Mr. Westworth!"

"Rowena, whatever is the matter?"

"Let me go please, sir," she begged, struggling against his strong grip.

"Come now. Let's get out of this storm and you can tell me all about what's going on."

Mr. Westworth gently pulled Rowena around the corner she had just rounded, despite her protests. He stopped dead when he saw what she had been fleeing from. Rowena's grandmother hovered inches from the ground before him. She looked older, dried-out and brown, and wearing a tattered white dress. Her eye sockets were empty, as if her eyes had been eaten by worms long ago. Even still, they seemed to glare at the pair standing before her.

"Grandma!" Rowena squeaked.

The old woman peeled back her lips in a snarl, exposing yellow, sharply pointed teeth.

Mr. Westworth pulled Rowena behind him.

The woman struck Mr. Westworth hard with clawed hands, scratching his cheek and drawing blood from four parallel cuts. Rowena screamed.

With a desperate kick, Mr. Westworth sent the phantom flying backwards. He spun about and pulled Rowena back around the corner at a dead run. "Run!"

Sobbing and clutching his hand, Rowena ran.

"Where are we going?" she yelled through the storm.

"I have an idea."

They ran out of the school grounds and passed the dilapidated shed that marked the border of a neighboring sheep farm.

"What the...?" Rowena asked incredulously as Mr. Westworth picked her up and helped her over the low stone wall bordering the sheep's paddock. Unperturbed by the intruders, the sheep stared and chewed on the soaking grass.

"Go!"

"Go where?"

"Straight! Run straight!"

Rowena's legs pounded the earth, and she glanced over her shoulder at Mr. Westworth as he caught up with her. He grasped her hand again, and they ran to a large, fenced off square in the centre of which stood a small stone circle. They reached the edge of the circle, and Mr. Westworth grabbed her by the shoulders.

"Do you have the key?" he asked.

"What? Why?"

"Just answer me! Do you have it?"

*We're being chased across the country by something out of a bad horror film, and he wants my key?* She fumbled in her coat pockets and, for a moment, feared she left it behind. Relief flooded through Rowena when her fingers curled around the metal, and she pulled the key out.

"I saw your mother use a key like the one you had today here, once."

Rowena looked up at him in surprise.

"It was a long time ago. I was just a young lad, no more than seventeen. I thought it had been a dream. Time does not move the same in her world. I thought she was just a dream. Rowena Fae…"

"What is it?" Rowena asked. Mr. Westworth's expression clouded as he struggled with himself a moment. Then his face set in resolve.

"I'm sending you home." He pushed her roughly into the circle. "I dare not go further. Hold onto that key, Rowena, and sing."

"What?"

"Sing, Rowena! Sing!"

The phantom glided over the paddock, sending the sheep into a frenzied panic. Rowena opened her mouth and tried to sing. Her throat was so dry that no sound came from it at first. Rowena looked into Mr. Westworth's kind eyes. He smiled at her, and Rowena found her voice again. Shaky at first, but it grew stronger as the song began to take shape. Planxty Lady Wrixon, her favorite tune.

Rowena watched in surprise as the stones of the circle began to glow. Faintly at first, and then it became a warm, honey color as the key began its crystalline singing in response to Rowena's own music.

"Give my love to your mother," he called as the glowing intensified.

The phantom woman reached the edge of the stone circle. Rowena watched helplessly as Mr.

Westworth turned to face her, his hands raised in defense. The phantom raised one clawed hand high and brought it down hard on his head.

Rowena screamed. She never saw him hit the ground. The bright glow flared, blinding her.

When she could see again, she found herself in the stone circle, but the fence had vanished. In place of stone walls and sheep, open grassland, greener than she could ever have imagined, rolled in gentle waves to the horizon. The sun shone brightly, and birds sang as they flew overhead.

After a few minutes, she noticed a young woman, dressed in a long, flowing red dress tied at the shoulders with ornate gold clasps standing on the edge of the circle. Rowena stared at her. She was the most beautiful thing Rowena had ever seen. It took her a moment longer to realize she recognized the woman standing before her.

"Mother?"

The woman smiled and opened her arms to Rowena. Rowena stumbled forward, fear and relief making her legs next to useless, and sank gratefully into the woman's embrace.

"Oh my child," the woman said. She laughed through her tears. "It's alright now. You are home now. You are safe."

"What happened? To me? To Grandma?"

"It was Samhain when you stumbled into the circle," Rowena's mother said. "And it was too late when we realized what had happened. You were but four years old then and had no way to return. We sent Doris through to look after you until you were old enough to...to come home."

"Doris?"

"You called her 'Grandma.'"

Rowena's eyes filled with tears as she remembered the kindly old woman who had looked after her since she could remember, and the terrible phantom that had masqueraded as her.

"What happened to her?"

"The Fir Bolg have long used dark magic to hunt us. Poor Doris. Her sacrifice was greater than any we could have imagined."

"Why didn't she tell me?"

"Sweet child, no one is allowed into the Land of the Sid unless they can prove themselves pure of heart. It was a secret that had to be kept until you were ready to know; to preserve your innocence, or you would never have been able to come back. And this land needs its princess. Oh," her mother sobbed, "look how beautiful you've become." She pulled Rowena close once more. "I have missed you so."

Rowena pulled back and smiled up at her mother. Her mother's raven black hair fell straight to her shoulders, but her eyes were a startling blue.

"You look just like I did at your age," Rowena's mother said, as if guessing Rowena's thoughts. "But for your eyes. Green as spring grass, and sparkling like dew in the morning sun. You have your father's eyes."

# ABOUT THE AUTHORS

# JAIMEY GRANT

J aimey Grant was born in Michigan in 1979, the fourth of five children. Childhood passed in a blur of humid summers and freezing, snowy winters.

She started writing after devouring hundreds of traditional Regency romances. She used to believe it took some kind of genius to write a book. Knowing she was not a genius, she decided to try anyway. After sitting down with a set of characters and a basic plot, she wrote her first book from start to finish. It wasn't perfect or even good by any means, but it was still something to be proud of.

Over a dozen manuscripts later, she finally considers herself to be a writer.

Currently residing in Michigan with her husband and two children, she is working on several more Regency romances.

**Blogs and sites:**
http://www.jaimeygrant.com/
http://jaimeygrant.blogspot.com/
http://www.goodreads.com/jaimeygrant

# WENDY SWORE

In Pocatello, Idaho, Wendy's summers are spent working on the family truck farm along with their five young children. After the sweet-corn harvest, thousands of people come to learn about agriculture in her educational corn maze and farm tours.

Wendy makes time for writing/editing every day year round, and twice as much in the winter when farming is over.

Two of her short stories are available as free downloads in the Ménage à 20 anthology published December 2009 with the combined efforts of 20 goodreads.com authors.

About her projects currently in the works, Wendy says, "My first YA novel follows Jenna, a farm girl, as she struggles against a lurking menace on the Sho-Ban Indian reservation. It's in the query process right now. My next is a dystopia that deals with slavery and a young girl's race against the destruction of her people."

**Blogs and sites:**
http://wendyswore.blogspot.com
http://www.goodreads.com/wendyswore

# RITA J. WEBB

**T**hroughout her childhood, Rita J. Webb travelled around the country with a book always in hand. She finally settled in Ohio where she attended college to study Computer Science and then began a career as a Software Test Analyst, a beautiful title for an empty position.

Rita's love for books and great stories pushed her to start writing when impending layoffs forced her to reconsider her dreams and goals. Having tested software for ten years, she wanted to create something more meaningful than a test manual, something that would move hearts.

With her husband TJ, Rita home-schools her three girls, who keep her busy with art, science projects, books to read, and walks about the park.

**Blogs and sites:**
http://afantasyfiction.blogspot.com
http://www.goodreads.com/ritajwebb
rita@ritajwebb.com

# PAIGE RAY

**P**aige Ray, age 26, lives with her husband and three-year-old son in Central California. Currently, Paige and her family are considering a move to the redwood-covered coast of Northern California.

She is an avid reader, reading up to three books a week. Writing is her favorite pastime, though she has yet to finish a full novel. She is in a collaborative writing group that is working on a novel to be published in 2011, and she has recently been contacted by a literary agent in regards to a short story she has written. She is a frequent blogger with book reviews, aspiring author interviews, and an occasional look into her life.

She used to be a plethora of job titles at an electrical construction firm, but a family move gave her the idea to be a stay-at-home mom and educate her son as best she could before he starts school. This is where she found reading and writing again, after an absence of several years. She loves every minute of it.

**Blogs and sites:**
http://www.paigeray.blogspot.com
http://www.twitter.com/PortlandPaige23
http://www.goodreads.com/paigeray
paigeray23@yahoo.com

# JEANNE VOELKER

J eanne Voelker spent her childhood years in the foothills of the Cascade Mountains. She graduated from the University of Washington, Seattle, in 1980 with a degree in English literature. She studied literature and composition because she considers stories essential to life.

She has always admired a well-told tale, and for many years, stories have amused, encouraged, educated, and sustained her. Now it's her turn to add to the pot. She writes from her remodeled farmhouse in Seattle where she also has a well-established tutoring business.

**Blogs and sites:**

http://www.goodreads.com/jeanne_voelker

# K. G. BORLAND

**K**yle G. Borland was born in Massachusetts but has lived half his life in Europe and the other half all over the US. Kyle has had a love of writing for a long time. His first published piece was last year in the Blue Moon Literary & Art Review's Fall-Winter Edition 2009 for his short story, Banishment.

Now residing in Alabama, Kyle lives with his parents and his black lab, Chloe.

He is a senior in high school but hopes to complete his final year early. When asked about graduating early, Kyle says, "I want to have that time that would be the second semester as a time to write and travel. I feel ahead of the game trying to get published this young. Hopefully, I keep that feeling and make the best out of this up-and-coming year."

Kyle is currently working on his first full length novel.

**Blogs and sites:**

http://kgborland23.blogspot.com/
http://www.goodreads.com/kgborland

# GWENDOLYN MCINTYRE

Gwendolyn McIntyre was born in the United Kingdom but has lived most of her life either in the USA or traveling the globe, trying to do good works.

Gwen is a writer, editor, educator and business woman who lives with her partner Melissa, their ninety-five pound Staffordshire Bull Terrier 'other child', and a host of other animals and creatures... both real and imaginary.

**Blogs and sites:**

http://britishimport.livejournal.com
http://medicinewoman.wordpress.com
http://www.goodreads.com/drgwen

# KATRINA MONROE

**K**atrina is a writer, avid reader, pretend painter, and mother of two. After finding a new love in short stories and flash fiction (the gatos thank you, Henry and Renee), she's found that writing can not only be a great creative outlet, but a freaking blast, too.

**Blogs and sites:**

http://do-as-i-say-and-nonsense.blogspot.com
http://www.goodreads.com/katrinalee

# S. M. CARRIÈRE

**B**orn in Quito, Ecuador, raised in Australia and now living in Canada, S. M. Carrière has found a passion and direction she never thought possible in writing. Growing up, she never thought she would strive to become an author. That is precisely what she is doing now, however.

The first book she'd ever written, a fantasy novel, turned into a four book series (The Great Man) and was completed in August 2009. She is now trying desperately to have published the first book of the series (The Third Prince). Since then she has written two more full length novels in a separate series (The Seraphime Saga), also fantasy, and has two other stories in the boiler.

With 6 completed novels and two completed series, she thinks she can safely call herself a writer! The trick is getting them published...

**Blogs and sites:**
http://smcarriere.blogspot.com/
http://www.goodreads.com/smcarriere

CPSIA information can be obtained at www.ICGtesting.com
Printed in the USA
BVOW03s1210171114

375441BV00026B/277/P